METROPOLICKS Book 3:
Love is Everywhere

Felicia Lin and Victor Scott Rodriguez

WWS Press
New York

WWS Press
Metropolicks Book 3: Love is Everywhere
Felicia Lin and Victor Scott Rodriguez

Published in the United States of America by WWS Press
ISBN 978-0-9996179-9-1

Printed by Create Space, a DBA of On-Demand Publishing LLC

Metropolicks*
[mi-trop-uh-liks]

noun

1. A large, busy international city (e.g. New York City) filled with varied stories of relationship adventures and misadventures.

2. A major urban center in which sexual activity is prominent, especially those involving the use of one's tongue.

3. A fast-paced, competitive metropolis where highly ambitious people focus on licking the competition and getting ahead in dating.

* as defined on The Urban Dictionary

FOR MORE ON METROPOLICKS VISIT: www.Metropolicks.com

ACKNOWLEDGMENTS

Writing a book is one thing, but creating a finished product is another. There are indeed many people to thank and acknowledge for making this book series happen. It is hard to know where to begin.

Thank you to Alice Heiserman, our diligent, enthusiastic content and copy editor, who added much value to the novel. We owe you a great deal.

We'd also like to acknowledge the contributions of those who gave us insights, each in their own way, into the mechanics and legalities of self-publishing: Hugh Howey, Guy Kawasaki and Shawn Welch, Maria Murnane, and Rob Thony.

Many thanks to the several romance authors who shared their experience and advice with us including: Tina DeSalvo, Debra Holland, Beverly Jenkins, Diane Kelly, Maggie Marr, Tessa McFionn, Sarah MacLean, Priscilla Oliveras, Maggie Rivers, and Cecilia Tan.

Much appreciation goes to those who offered advice and recommendations regarding the cover designs of the book series, among them are: Candace Braun Davison, Serena Chen, Joanne Louie, Johanna Salazar, and Peter Yang Zhao.

We are grateful to Vinny Bove, Emily Chen, George Madarasz, and Michelle Shinagawa for your recommendations and expertise in making our book covers come to life. A big thank you also goes to Gilly Rosenthol, who formatted our book series. We'd also like to thank Jennie Yip and Claudine Lee who created a one-of-a-kind artwork that appears in the Metropolicks ebook.

A big debt of thanks goes to Maggie Law, our talented photographer, who tirelessly photographed several models during a marathon shoot. Among the models are: Jide Alao, Sarah Clark, Ryan Dawalt, Mieko Gavia, Jason He, Lynda Hinder, Kara Xinhang Li, Andrew Nicholas, Prakash Patil, David Rodriguez, Gabby Jiayin She, Tina Telalyan, and Pai-Sen Wang. Each one of you brought something truly unique to the shoot and your photos have been used for our promotional campaigns. But we do want to especially thank Davide Filippini and Sheila G., our Metropolicks Books 1-3 cover models. The chemistry between the two of you, as seen in your photos and the Metropolicks videos, is undeniable. Other people to thank regarding the photo shoot include: Kristin Mirabelle, our hair and makeup artist, Alice Chin, our wardrobe consultant, and the rest of the crew: Huaying Chen, Deanna Denman, Annie Lu, Sara Vinik, and Tony Wong.

We are grateful to Jami Jackson, Caesar Jackson and Blacque Records for sharing Jami's musical talent with us. Jami's songs "Let Love Live" and "Keep Walkin' On" have been featured in two Metropolicks music videos with the behind the scenes footage from the photo shoot.

And before all of this, there were our test readers. Thank you; you were the first ones to give us feedback and perspective on the novel.

We also want to specifically acknowledge the following people for their support and friendship: Juan Betancourt, David Chan, Will Chao, Nicole Chen, Donna Drake, Diana Lee, Jack Li, Supei Liu, Joanne Louie, Diana Mao, Alissa Moore, Chris Nicodemo, Krista Sande-Kerback, Nelson Searcy, Ryan Shemen, Jim Su, Kerrick Thomas, Lorie Thomas, Yue Wang, and Cindy Zhou.

And lastly, thank you to Catarina Serra and Ichi Shih for hosting a Halloween party several years ago, where we met each other for the very first time. The rest, as they say, is history.

Felicia and Victor

TABLE OF CONTENTS

METROPOLICKS DEFINITION 3

ACKNOWLEDGMENTS 4

INTRODUCTION.. 9

YEAR III: SPRING

The Appeal of the Unattainable
(LUANA and Katia) 15

The Growth Group
(MONTOYA and Nine)... 19

A Woman's Comfort Zone
(NINE)... 27

The Non-Date Date
(TARA) 32

Overnight
(NINE)... 38

The Elusive Double Date
(MONTOYA) 44

YEAR III: SUMMER

The Good, The Bad, and The Tantric
(LUANA) 49

In This Life and the Next
(FRANK) 52

Don't Forget the Girlfriend
(MONTOYA) 58

Totally Resistible
(ROXANNE and Tara) 63

Saying I Do
(MONTOYA and Nine) 67

Rivers to Cross
(TARA) 71

Angels with Clean Faces
(TARA) 78

Through the Eyes of a Child
(TARA) 83

Time Stands Still
(TARA) 90

YEAR III: FALL

Not Tempting Karma
(FRANK) 101

It's All About Improvement
(KATIA and Luana) 104

Alternate Reality
(NINE and Montoya) 109

One Scoop or Two?
(TARA and Roxanne) 113

The Toy Chest
(LUANA) 120

Men, You Can't Live With Them or Without Them
(LUANA) 124

Doing It Without Doing It
(LUANA) 128

YEAR III: WINTER

Gentlemen Prefer (   )?
(TARA) 135

Grow Up Already
(ROXANNE) 140

Two Condoms are Better than One
(FRANK and Montoya) 145

Who Needs a Storybook Wedding?
(Nine, Montoya, Tara, Luana, Frank,
Katia, and Roxanne) 149

The Burning Bush
(NINE) 157

EPILOGUE 162

INTRODUCTION

Dating in New York is not for the faint of heart. With so many singles packed into the island of Manhattan and people marrying later in life, you'd think that there would be endless opportunities to find love. However, with so many options, it is easy to find yourself going through the revolving doors of dating. There are always fresh distractions—the newer, the better, or the trendier. Who has the time or patience to make relationships work? So, are the odds really in your favor in New York if you are looking for Mr. or Ms. Right?

To have a fighting chance you'll need a plan of attack and a support system. In fact, you'll need all the help you can get. You'll need an army to win this war. This army includes your friends, those you can trust, those who you can go to with the joy and the pain of your pursuit. Don't forget your friends' friends, and your acquaintances—you never know who you'll meet through these connections. And then, you will need a backup plan. So, suit up, put on your best armor—be it a little black dress or your sharpest looking suit. Lock and load your best pickup lines or your sexiest, most charming smile, because love is a battlefield. And as the saying goes, you may have to kiss a lot of frogs before you find your prince or princess.

When you are single and have lived in New York long enough, you will probably have a few stories to share. We soon found out that this was truer than we could have imagined. As friends heard that we were working on this novel, a strange thing began happening. People started volunteering to share their dating stories with us.

While our novel was inspired in part by people's true dating experiences in New York City, these experiences were used in a fictitious manner. The novel is a work of fiction and is a result of our creative imagination. Our intention was to create characters who were composites. Therefore, any resemblance to real persons, living or dead, is purely coincidental and unintentional.

Another unusual development happened during the writing of this book—when someone gave us legal consent to be mentioned in the book by name, with the caveat that none of that individual's personal stories be included in the book. That led to several other people being mentioned in the book by their real names, and we followed the same protocol with each of them. Thus, the stories in this book are interspersed with the names of real people and real places.

There are many stories to be told and others that are best kept private. We are here to tell the tales of a few New Yorkers brave enough to endure heartbreak and rejection in order to find love. In the words of the great poet Ovid, "Fortune and love favor the brave."

We wish to thank all who have contributed stories, but, of course, we can't do so by name. In order to protect people's anonymity, we have changed names, ethnicities, occupations, places of residence and identifiable physical characteristics, and in some instances, the gender, national origin, religious views, and political views of those who have volunteered stories. In every instance, we have combined several stories within the same chapter, so that every chapter is in fact composite in nature.

One last thought: when a dating relationship goes awry, don't sweat it; it is not the end of the world. How do we know it is not the end of the world? Because it is already tomorrow in Taiwan.

YEAR III

_____

SPRING

The Appeal of the Unattainable
(LUANA and Katia)

Katia and I were at an exclusive party on Park Avenue. The event was the after party for the release of the *Sports Illustrated Swimsuit Edition*. Johanna, a socialite originally from Brazil, was the hostess. Among the guests at the event were many sports figures and, of course, the models from the *Swimsuit Edition*. I knew several of the Brazilian models personally and was chatting with them as a short man with a receding hairline approached. That was Tommy. As he stood beside most of the models, he was eye level with their chests or in some cases their stomachs. He looked up at them while he attempted to engage them in conversation. I excused myself and went to talk to Katia, who had just finished giving her number to a sports agent.

"Why does Johanna invite Tommy to these parties?" Katia asked. "Look at him, hitting on the models. It is embarrassing."

"I agree but he is a good friend of Johanna. He was the one who helped her get her first job when she first came to this country and needed a job. He was also her green card sponsor and helped her meet her ex, who was loaded. She was set up for life after the divorce and she's never forgotten what Tommy did for her," I explained.

"While I admire loyalty to friends, let's get real. What chance does he have with these models? What is he? Five feet tall? He is too short to shop in the men's departments of stores. He would have to shop in the boys' section or get his suits custom made. Is he at least good in bed?" Katia asked.

"He is a millionaire although I wouldn't say he is super rich. I did hear from Johanna that he is good in bed. Johanna had given him a test ride before she had married her ex. I think he and Johanna still might do it every once in a while."

"Still, he only likes super tall models. Look at the two of us. Most men would die to have us as their girlfriends and yet this putz wouldn't want us because we aren't six feet tall. Tonight he thinks he hit the jackpot, so he is trying to approach every single tall model here," Katia said observantly.

"Yes, and they are politely or sometimes not so politely telling him to bug off. I've seen him do this at several of Johanna's parties. What is amazing is that he doesn't change his preference to have more realistic standards. He is rich and good in bed. If he changed his height requirements for women, he would be sleeping with a gorgeous woman every night of the week," I added.

Katia took a sip of her champagne as she said, "Well, his relentless pursuit of the unattainable is getting annoying to watch."

"Yes, I've seen him do this time and time again. So, now, I just ignore him totally. Not even a kiss on the cheek. I hold out my hand for him to shake, which from me is the kiss of death for any man. I kiss everyone on the cheek. If I hold out my hand, you have to be an idiot not to get it that I don't like you," I said agreeing with Katia.

I took a piece of sushi from one of the tables laden with food and added, "I have a colleague, Betsy, who doesn't date at all because she hasn't met a man who meets her criteria. She is from San Francisco and her ideal man is at least 5'10," likes to travel and enjoys Broadway musicals and ballet. So far, she hasn't found him, but in her mind, this man is out there."

"I want a good looking man with money who caters to my needs. Very simple. Good looking, money, generous, and teachable. There are actually many men like that. It is just finding the right fit for me. However, there are many people like Tommy and Betsy who are looking for this needle-in-a-haystack potential mate. They have a laundry list in their head of all the qualities this person should have and they don't believe in compromising whatsoever. So, they won't even date unless someone meets their criteria. Not many even make it to the first date. To me it seems insane," Katia said and then took another sip of her champagne.

"They say that the definition of insanity is doing the same thing over and over and expecting a different result. So I'd agree that constantly looking for an unrealistic ideal seems kind of insane," I responded.

Katia waved her champagne glass in the air as she said, "My advice for these ladies is don't care about whether or not the man likes opera or ballet or show tunes... do that with your women friends."

"And don't care if he is the same height as you or a little shorter, if you want a guy who is taller, just wear flats," I added. "Don't care if he has a receding hairline. I say, trust me ladies, those firm tits of yours will be influenced by gravity sooner than you would like. All of our bodies get older."

"But the one non-negotiable is that he has to have money. Without money, you might as well fill out the divorce papers when you say your marriage vows," Katia said laughing.

I laughed, too, and then said, "I would add that a woman should find a man who truly cares for her, someone who can be her partner, satisfies her in bed, is decent, and has a good heart. The rest is not important. As for myself, I have had a hard time finding a good guy. But it's not because I am searching for the perfect man. I like variety and I don't know if I can be faithful forever to one man—no matter how good looking or good in bed he is. I have been married already. So, I'm not necessarily looking for marriage but the thought of having a child is appealing. I'm not looking so much for a husband, what I want is someone to have a baby with. I don't believe in finding some 'happily ever after' like in a fairy tale."

"In the meanwhile, you seem to be happy in your search. I am sure you could easily leave this party with one of these football stars," Katia said to me.

"Well, that is true and whenever I find a decent enough guy who isn't right for me, I sort of pass him on to my girlfriends. Maybe they can do something with him that I couldn't," I paused a moment and then added, "This reminds me of this urologist I met a while ago. Pathetic in bed. Terrible kisser. But good looking and sitting on a pile of money. I thought he was beyond hope. I just don't have the patience to deal with someone so inexperienced with women. But maybe you could do something with him."

"Is he taller than Tommy?" Katia asked in jest.

"Yes, I think this might work. You can mold him as you see fit. As you've said before, you like them dumb and rich."

Just then, one of the New York Giants football players approached me. Katia gave me a knowing look and a glib smile.

The Growth Group

(MONTOYA and Nine)

A few weeks after our return from Israel, I finally visited Nine's church, The Journey, for their 1 P.M. service. Nine explained that The Journey doesn't actually own a central building, so they'd rent out different places and because of that, the location would periodically change. For the next few months, they were going to be meeting in Caroline's Comedy Club, which may seem unusual for a church gathering, but when I arrived, I saw that it was fitting since they opened up their services with rock music and multi-media visuals.

After the service, Nine and I stepped out. There were coffee, donuts, and assorted pastries on a table outside. I grabbed a jelly donut and Nine took a blueberry muffin. We each then got a cup of coffee.

"So, what did you think of the service?" Nine asked.

"I liked it a lot. The sermon was good and offered practical advice. The rock music was surprisingly good and some of the women here are very attractive," I said.

"Did your religious experience in Jerusalem say that you should go back to church for the women?" Nine said making fun of me.

"Well, who knew such gorgeous women went to church?" I asked raising my coffee cup in a mock toast.

"Montoya, you have always been such a ladies' man, but you have a good heart. I think you need to meet some different types of women. Come to the church growth group that I am co-leading."

"You mean your Bible study group?" I said now poking fun at Nine.

"Come on, I've told you before that we study a Christian book and discuss it. We also share prayer requests with each other. And, as an added bonus, you could meet a nice, cute Christian woman."

"Hey, you just got me to start going to church again, but you think I should go for a holy roller now?"

"Believe me, it is harder to find a good Christian guy than it is to find a good Christian woman. The women outnumber the men. And what's wrong with being with a Christian woman? Am I a holy roller? You can meet women like me. If you weren't one-hundred years older than me, maybe I would date you," Nine said laughing.

"One-hundred years! Very funny. It's more like a ten-year age difference. Of course, I would date someone from your church if she was a nice, pretty, and fun woman like you, not some religious nut."

"So, just come to the growth group that I am co-leading with my friend Joy Chang. We are meeting in my apartment."

"Okay, Nine. I will give it a try."

Two days later I showed up at Nine's apartment for her Tuesday growth group. Gone were the old boxes of pizza, used cartons of Chinese food, and crumpled balls of tissue. Since our trip to Jerusalem, Nine had been lifted out of her depression. She seemed to have a positive outlook on life.

A lovely Asian woman greeted me at the door when I arrived. I soon found out she was Joy, Nine's co-leader of the group. The first thing I noticed about her was that she had a warm and friendly smile. She also had beautiful hair that reached just below her shoulders. I could tell that she had a great figure even though she was dressed simply in a fitted T-shirt and jeans.

As I looked around the room, I saw that ten people were already there. Some people were engaging in friendly conversation and others were sitting quietly waiting. I found everyone to be somewhat laid back. After another seven people arrived, Joy and Nine started talking to the group. First, they directed everyone in doing some icebreakers so we could get to know each other. Then, we went over what would be happening at the meeting each week. We would be discussing *Mere Christianity*, a book by C. S. Lewis, and after that, at the end of each meeting the group would be taking prayer requests.

Nine had told me ahead of time about the book so I had spent some time reading it. I found it interesting that C. S. Lewis made the argument early on in the book, that having a conscience was proof of the existence of God. He made me see things in a different light. When it came time for me to make a prayer request, I asked for help to get over my resentful feelings toward God. I had a chance to talk to several people that night, but it was Joy who stood out. I still remember the conversation clearly.

"Nine told me a little bit about your situation," Joy said to me.

"Really?" I said wondering just what Nine had said to Joy.

Seeing the look on my face, Joy said, "She didn't tell me any personal details. She just said that you were away from church for many years. If you don't mind, I'd like to suggest some books for you to help you grow as a Christian."

"Okay," I said somewhat surprised by her forwardness.

"I would recommend that you read *Disappointment with God* by Philip Yancey, *The Prodigal God* by Tim Keller, as well as Rick Warren's *The Purpose Driven Life*."

After writing myself a note on my mobile phone with all of her suggestions, I said, "Thanks for the suggestions. So, does every growth group do the same book at the same time?"

"No. The leader of each group picks a book to discuss from a variety of Christian authors. The Journey has about one hundred growth groups running concurrently. Each growth group meets for a thirteen-week period, three times a year. This gives people the opportunity to try different groups throughout the year and to meet new people. In between each thirteen-week period, there's a one-month break, so that people have some down time. During the icebreaker, you mentioned that this is your first time at a growth group. So, what do you think?" Joy asked.

"Yes, I am a growth group virgin, so remember to be gentle with me," I joked. "But seriously, I did enjoy it."

"Ah, a comedian."

"Well, I try to be funny. You said during the icebreaker that this was the sixth growth group that you have co-led and the third time co-leading specifically with Nine. As you are so experienced, maybe you can teach me a thing or two," I said attempting to flirt with Joy.

"I've been going to The Journey for three years now. In that time has Nine managed to get you to go to The Journey with her?" she asked apparently not picking up on my flirting.

"I don't attend regularly. I only went once. This may be my first and last time at the growth group."

"Well, if you don't come back, I would be very sad about it. You wouldn't want me to be sad, now, would you?" she asked in a way that made me think that now she was flirting with me.

"Really, you would miss me? I now feel very special," I teased back.

So, that's how it started. I went back the next week and talked some more to Joy. She was in her mid-thirties and had only recently become a Christian. She had come to the United States from Singapore ten years ago. She was a librarian at Columbia University, and her smile and laugh were infectious. I asked her out for a drink but she said she was busy that week. The next week, I asked again, and she was still busy, but she said she'd take a rain check. When I asked her a third time the following week, she said she might be able to fit me into her schedule.

"So, are you playing hard to get? Or are you just flirting with me so that I come back each week?" I asked.

"I was wondering, Sherlock, when you would figure it out. I got you to come back three times, so you must really want to have that drink with me. You must be very thirsty by now."

"Do you do this to all the guys in the group?"

"No, just the growth group virgins who have the name Montoya and who speak with a British accent," she said as she tossed her head back with a big laugh.

"That is very specific."

"Actually, you keep asking me for a drink, but I really don't drink that much. But I do love sushi. That's a hint. Not tonight though. I have to be at school early in the morning. But how about dinner after the evening church service on Sunday?"

"So, you are asking me out? I didn't think Christian women were that forward."

"Actually, you look like you could use a little 'Joy' in your life," was her snappy comeback.

I fancied her quick wit.

That Sunday at the end of the service, Joy introduced me to the Pastor of The Journey Manhattan, Kerrick Thomas. Pastor Kerrick had joked during the sermon that you had to be smart to attend The Journey, since only smart, resourceful people would be able find the church from week to week. Joy told me that in the past, The Journey had their services in a grand ballroom of a hotel, in a public school and sometimes in other churches.

I always thought ministers were supposed to be old, but Kerrick was younger than me. He greeted me with a sincere smile and handshake and introduced me to his wife, Lorie, with whom I had a long conversation. I glanced sideways to see Joy watching us with a wide grin on her face.

I remembered that Joy had hinted that she liked sushi, so I suggested a Japanese place for lunch. Joy ordered the salmon avocado with brown rice and I ordered the special otoro sushi which was the tender, fatty underbelly of the blue fin tuna. After we ordered our food, I was still thinking about the grin on Joy's face earlier, so I said to her, "I saw you grinning at me as I was talking to Lorie. Was it because you saw that I liked talking to the minister's wife?"

"No, it's because you saw her as a person and not as a stereotype."

"I have to admit both the minister and his wife seemed very sincere in their beliefs. Since you mentioned that you've only been a Christian for three years, I'm wondering, how did you make that decision?"

"Well, The Journey has had a big part in it. One day as I was walking down the street, I was given a granola bar and a flyer about The Journey. That's how I found out about them three years ago. Shortly after that, I started attending the church. In the first year, I met Nine and after I got baptized, she and I decided to co-lead a growth group together. I have really benefited from her friendship," Joy explained.

"Lately, I have really benefited from my friendship with her also. Very much so. But it started out with me being her mentor at work. But as a Christian, she is definitely going to be my mentor. Unless, of course, you want that job?" I said hoping she would pick up on my flirting again.

The waiter came with our food, and as I reached for my chopsticks, Joy interrupted me by putting her hand on mine.

"Let's say grace together," Joy said.

"Okay," I responded.

After she said a brief prayer of thanks, I resumed my previous train of thought.

"Actually, Nine was partially responsible for getting me to go back to church," I said and then paused. "And now you seem to have taken up part of that responsibility as well."

"Yes, with pleasure," Joy said this time obviously flirting.

"So it's not my imagination that you've lured me into coming back to the growth group every week."

"Lured? I just flirted with you and you took the bait."

"Okay, yes, you flirted with me. I'm wondering what is it that made you take an interest in me so quickly?"

"Nine said you were one of the best men she has ever met. How much better of a reference can a person have?"

I guess I passed the test with Joy because she finally agreed to go on second date with me. It was to see the re-release of *The Lion King* movie in 3D. I wasn't sure where this relationship would go but the movie's message was very fitting, "Don't worry. Be happy."

Later on, back at home, I thought of my life for the past two decades and how much time I had lost in developing my relationship with God. Meeting Joy made me realize that my life had become a version of the Prodigal Son's story in the Bible. I had heard the story so many times at church growing up and it went in one ear and out the other. But now, I realized that it had become my story—a young man who rejected his father and went off to a life of promiscuity. Then, the young man finally came to his senses and went back to his father, who symbolically represented God. All that was missing in my case was the fatted calf, which was cooked to celebrate the young man's homecoming. I don't eat red meat, so instead I had the otoro fatty tuna sushi.

I also thought about Joy. I had never dated a Christian woman before. I didn't know if it would work out or how far to go physically with her. All of this was uncharted territory for me. But I now felt reconnected to God and realized that He would be there guiding me in this relationship with Joy. Tears came to my eyes as I looked out my window and up to the sky and said, "Thank you, Evie. After twenty years, your Archie bear has finally come home."

Meanwhile, there was another new addition to the growth group, Kristof Eklund. He was a financial advisor, who had recently moved to Manhattan via Stockholm. I could tell that most of the women in the group thought he was cute, but there was something subtle about the way he interacted with Nine that made me think he might be interested in her.

I bought a *One Year Bible*, which is a Bible that is broken up into 365 daily readings. Every day I'd read a bit of it. Joy and I would sit together each week at The Journey's evening service in the Village. When I told my parents that I was back in church and reading The Bible again, my Mum cried.

A Woman's Comfort Zone

(NINE)

I usually can tell when a guy is interested in me, but with Kristof I didn't see it coming. He'd been attending the growth group I co-led with Joy for several weeks. He had just joined the group not long after moving to New York from Stockholm, and he had this newcomer vibe. After living in New York for a while, it's easy to spot newcomers. They have this openness to meeting people, trying new things, and experiencing all that New York City has to offer.

Kristof had a very European style, which seemed intriguing, sophisticated, and foreign. I think it was because he had never lived outside of Europe before. I could tell that many of the women in the group found him attractive. It was hard not to notice the combination of his chiseled looks, gray-blue eyes, dirty blonde hair, and tall stature. Since Kristof was so approachable and open to talking to people, it was difficult to tell if he had already taken an interest in any of the women in the group. I thought it would only be a matter of time before one of the women snagged him, or perhaps he'd already taken an interest in someone specific.

A few times, he'd stayed behind chatting with someone at the end of the meeting and each time he offered to help Joy and me clean up. Of course, we told him it wasn't necessary, but he just started picking up the paper plates and cups and taking them to the kitchen. He even offered to take out the trash one time.

One evening as people were leaving, I overheard him chatting with Joy asking about her experiences as a growth group leader and in running a group. So, seeing my opportunity, I joined the conversation and asked him, "I couldn't help but overhear your conversation. Are you perhaps interested in co-leading a group yourself in the future?"

Joy had given me a sly smile and said to Kristof, "Excuse me a minute as I run to the restroom. I'll leave you to talk to Nine about this. She is the more experienced of the two of us." Then, she walked off leaving me alone with Kristof.

Picking up where we left off, Kristof said to me, "To answer your question, I'm not sure of that yet. I think I need to find the right co-leader. But you are already taken."

"No, I'm not taken!" I had blurted out. As soon as I'd heard the words come out of my mouth I felt embarrassed.

"Joy is lucky," Kristof had said, smiling as he said this. It was then I realized the entirety of what he had said and felt even more embarrassed. But then he said, "Well now that I know that you are not taken, I have no excuse to not ask you out. These past few weeks, I've been kind of hanging back, trying to figure out how I could ask you out. Can I call or email you about this later?"

He had caught me off guard. "Yes. That sounds good," I said feeling happy but cautious. Kristof was, after all, the first guy I'd be going on a date with since Rong and my trip to Israel.

After Kristof left, Joy told me that she had a feeling that Kristof had been working up the courage to ask me out.

On our first date, Kristof invited me to a Broadway show called *The First Date*, which seemed appropriate. However, the first date that happened in the play was a blind date. As we were having dessert and a drink together afterwards at a hotel bar overlooking Times Square, we each shared stories about awkward first dates.

"Even though this is our first date, it doesn't feel awkward at all because we've been kind of getting to know each other these past few weeks," Kristof commented.

After my crisis of faith and struggle over maintaining my virginity, I felt that I should set the tone for this relationship from the outset, so I said, "You're right. I'm curious to know what your approach to dating is, but first let me share mine. I am not the type to jump into the sack very quickly. Are you okay with that?"

"I sensed that about you. I knew that before I asked you out."

"I also don't believe in dating more than one person at the time. I think you should pick one person and see where it goes and it if goes in the right direction."

"We are on the same page, Nine. It does get too confusing trying to juggle dates. I prefer to focus on just one person, to really get to know her better."

After dessert, we walked south of Times Square. As we walked, Kristof reached over and held my hand. Before we knew it, we were in front of my apartment building in Union Square. He gave me a goodnight kiss on the lips. Then, I stood on the sidewalk waiting as he hailed a cab, and I watched him step into the cab before I turned to walk into my building. It was a wonderful first date. I went up to my apartment feeling hopeful.

Over the next several weeks, we went out once or twice a week aside from the night we had growth group. He was giving me real quality time and with each date I felt more comfortable with him and more trusting of his motives for being with me. It was so great to be with a man who wasn't only after one thing. One night, as the credits started rolling at the end of a movie that we'd been watching at my place, we started kissing on my sofa. As we stopped kissing, I reached for my glass of wine. I felt that it was time to open up to him. I started thinking about how to start this whole conversation and I hoped it wouldn't get too awkward.

"I really appreciate how you haven't pushed me to go past a certain point physically. It's important to me because I know that I want to wait to be with the man who I will spend the rest of my life with," I said and paused, waiting for his reaction.

"I see. I think it's important for you to know why I haven't pushed you. The first person I ever fell in love with while I was in college was this woman, Ingrid. She was Christian and we were very serious. After we were together for six months, I felt it was time to have sex. It was difficult for me to be with someone who I loved and was attracted to without being physically intimate," Kristof explained.

"How did she react to that?" I asked.

"She eventually gave in and at first she was okay with it. But then she started to have an incredible sense of guilt and started to feel like it ruined our relationship and that God wouldn't bless it anymore."

"That's horrible. But I can definitely understand the desire for physical intimacy when you care about someone. I have struggled with this since being a teenager. How did it end with her?"

"We started fighting about everything, and it seemed that we couldn't go back to where we were before we had sex. Ingrid finally decided to end the relationship and all contact with me. I felt devastated. I really thought she was the one. It made me realize that you have to really respect your partner's boundaries when it comes to sex and physical intimacy. Since then, I have been really careful not to go past a woman's comfort zone," Kristof said as he held my hand.

"So, would you like to know what is within my comfort zone?" I asked trying to muster the courage to lay it all out on the line.

"Of course, if you feel comfortable telling me."

"Well, I really don't normally share this with people. I am a virgin. I have never had sexual intercourse. I haven't been entirely pure though. But recently, I've resolved that I will wait for marriage." I'd said it aloud and now I couldn't take it back. The only other ex-boyfriend that I'd ever mentioned this to was Paul.

Kristof looked at me thoughtfully and said, "I respect that. But after what happened with Ingrid, I think once two people get past a certain point, the desire for intimacy is very strong."

"I agree. Of course, women desire intimacy as much as men. At some point, the two people need to decide if they are right for each other and ready to take the next step."

"So, let's take the next step," Kristof said as if he was making some sort of a declaration.

"You mean have sex?" I said thinking maybe I'd misjudged his motives.

"No," Kristof said in a way that told me he had sensed my apprehension. "What I meant by the next step is dating with a purpose. We need to be exclusive and really see if we are right for each other. How do you feel about that?"

"Oh, I'm a little embarrassed about what I just said. I guess it's just that when a man says he wants to take the next step, he usually means having sex."

Kristof looked at me for a moment and then he said, "You still haven't answered my question."

"I think I'm ready to take the next step then."

Later that evening, after Kristof had left, I realized how one-sided my past relationships had been. I had always been the one wanting to make each one work, but it takes two. This time, I'd finally met a man who was willing to take the time to make it work.

The Non-Date Date

(TARA)

Minh and I were having Sunday brunch at Le Pain Quotidien. We were long overdue for a girl chat session. The waiter brought Minh a pot of decaf and an open-faced turkey tartine sandwich. He brought me a vegetable quiche and a pot of regular coffee. It had been awhile since I'd seen Minh and I had something on my mind.

"The other day, I was on what I thought was a date, but the way it played out really leaves me wondering," I said to Minh.

"So what happened?" Minh asked as she reached to take a sip of her coffee.

"I went to the Thursday night Chelsea art gallery openings with the Art Lovers Meetup group that I belong to and afterward some of us went for dinner and drinks together. That's how I met this guy, Richard. I didn't think much of him at the time. He was this white guy of average looks and height, but he seemed nice enough, so I exchanged business cards with him at the end of the night. That night, he texted me saying that it was really great meeting me and that he wanted to keep in touch," I said.

"Oh, that's nice… if you're interested, that is," Minh said.

"Right. Well, then he started to text me daily saying things like 'Have a great day!' or 'Hope you're having a great day!' or 'Home from work yet?' Sometimes he'd text me little personal weather reports telling me that 'the weatherman says there's a chance of showers, make sure you have an umbrella.' "

"That sounds a bit annoying."

"Well, I thought it was kind of kind of cute and thoughtful actually. We exchanged a few friendly, flirty text messages," I explained.

"I know that you somehow ended up on a date with him, right? Did he finally pick up the damn phone and call you?" Minh asked trying to get to the point.

"Right, the text messaging went on for a few weeks and it was starting to get old. But then Richard suddenly emailed me saying that it had been so long since he'd seen me and that he'd like to get together. He said something about wanting to go to an art fair in Chelsea over the weekend. I had received a message that the Art Lovers Meetup group was planning to go and I thought he was referring to that. So, I asked if he was planning to go with the Meetup group. He responded that he didn't want to go in a group or to be rushed and that we should make it a date, just the two of us. I told him that I already had plans to have dinner that night with a friend visiting from D.C. but that my entire afternoon was free. He wrote me a few more emails to reconfirm our date and said that he was really looking forward to finally seeing me again."

"Great, so he finally actually asked you on a date," Minh paused. "Though, it was over email."

"Yes, and the date, which was last Saturday, turned out to be such a non-event, I don't even know what to call it."

"Why do you say that?"

"Well, I was supposed to meet Richard at noon at the art fair, but I was running late, so I called him to let him know I'd be fifteen minutes late. When I got there, he wasn't there so I texted him. He answered back that he was at another gallery and said he'd walk over. I waited and when I saw him, he seemed happy to see me and said, 'You look lovely' and gave me a hug. We walked into the building where the art fair exhibits were and were promptly told that there was a 10 dollar entrance fee. I was putting away my sunglasses and assumed that Richard would pay for me since it was a date after all."

"Right."

"I saw him take out a 20 dollar bill, and as he handed it over, he looked over to me as he took back his change and said, 'You have ten?'"

"That's ridiculous! I can't believe he didn't pay for you," Minh said surprised by this.

"I was a bit stunned and said, 'Yes,' took out my wallet and paid for myself. So, then we went in together and started looking at the exhibits. It was a bit awkward."

"Oh, you think?"

"Yeah. And not just that, it's often kind of awkward in these sorts of situations. I mean knowing how to pace yourself. Going to an art gallery or museum on a first date is probably not a good idea. How do you know how closely to walk with someone or how much space to give him? And some people like to linger as they look at different pieces."

"I see your point," Minh said waving her fork slightly as if to emphasize or note what I had said.

"Richard went ahead a bit looking at things, but I took my time going a bit more slowly, at my own pace. At some point, I was basically going through the exhibits by myself. Then, I saw Richard again and he asked if I had seen anything interesting, so I mentioned the Taiwanese artist's booth that I'd heard about. So, we went to look at it together."

Minh nodded as I continued, "Then he went off again and we lost track of each other once more. I looked around for him. I thought how hard could it be to find him? I mean the building that the art fair was in was basically a straight, long space. It's not like it had a complicated layout with different rooms or sectioned areas. So, when I reached the end of the exhibit I walked back to the front entrance to see if I could find him. Then, I thought that maybe if I stayed in one spot he'd eventually find me. As I was walking around, I heard some guy giving a presentation about digital porn. So, I thought, I'm curious and this is as good a spot as any to stay put at."

"Oh, and what would you have done if Richard found you listening to such a presentation?"

"I wasn't thinking about that, but I suppose it would have led to some interesting conversation. Anyhow, getting back to the digital porn presentation, which by the way was very good, the guy had this whole slideshow showing porn that everyday people are creating online."

"Really?" Minh asked while raising her eyebrows. "I'd be a bit embarrassed to stand in public staring at that sort of stuff. It's kind of hard to not look at it and be curious, but I'd rather keep that sort of thing to myself."

"It wasn't the type of porn that you're thinking of. Nothing hardcore. His message was that regardless of one's shape, size, color, age, race, or physical attributes, there's someone out there who wants you or fetishizes you. There are fetishes for everything. And not all of them are what you'd necessarily consider sexy or kinky, like for example, a sock fetish. Did you know that there are people posting photos of just their feet in socks online, for their throngs of admirers? It's not about nudity, exposing any skin or body parts at all."

"Oh… I was picturing something like what you'd see at the Museum of Sex."

"No, it wasn't like that at all. When the guy was done with his presentation, I realized that nearly twenty minutes had passed! I walked around some more to see if I could find Richard. Then, I texted him and even tried calling him, but he didn't pick up. I didn't know what happened to him."

"Seriously? Why wasn't he looking for you?" Minh said.

"Exactly. So, I left him a voicemail telling him that I was leaving. Later on that night, I also wrote him an email saying: 'I didn't know what happened to you. I couldn't find you, but I figured that you could have tried calling me if you were wondering where I was. But you didn't. That left me in a kind of awkward situation. So, I just decided to leave.' And I ended the email by saying, 'There's no need for any explanations, or apologies and no hard feelings.' " I paused, "I didn't want to leave things so awkward and I figured this would give him a chance to explain himself."

"So… did he ever respond back?" Minh asked. "It's just so odd that he disappeared on you."

"Nope, never heard from him again," I said.

"Tara, you are too nice. How do you put up with these guys? You went way of out of your way, emailing him afterward. I wouldn't have bothered to do that. I mean it's like he stood you up in the middle of your date!" Minh said feeling outraged. She always feels bad hearing about what I've gone through with some of these date duds.

"I suppose, I do wonder why he disappeared."

"Maybe he was upset that you had told him you were busy at night and just limited it to seeing him in the afternoon?" Minh suggested.

"I can't see how he could be. He was the one who suggested the date. People have afternoon first dates. Some first dates are just a coffee or a drink, or just brunch or lunch. I don't need to spend the entire day with him for it to be a date."

"You never know. Maybe he was not happy that you were late. And maybe that's why he made you cough up 10 dollars for your own admission to the art fair."

"Well, that's a possibility but he's the one that said it would be a date. I mean give me a break! That's such a passive-aggressive way to deal with things. Then to pull that disappearing act?! What's up with men? Do any of them know how to behave around women anymore?" I asked with some frustration.

"I guess they don't."

"I am not upset about it. Well, maybe I am a little disappointed. I am so confused by the male gender," I said.

"It sometimes seems like they are a different species, a totally different animal," Minh agreed.

I continued, "I don't know what to say about what happened with Richard. I'm calling it the non-date date. Why did I even bother with this guy? I didn't really think much of him at first, but then he was persistent. I guess that I was also kind of bored since I am not really seeing anyone special now. I thought I'd give him a chance."

"I think you should be more picky about who you give a chance to from now on," Minh advised.

"Well I won't be giving anyone a chance for a while since I've decided to go to Cambodia with the Nomi Network for a few weeks. I need a distraction from this latest dating slump and I've always wanted to go to Asia." Then, I added, "But on the bright side, that day at the art fair, I did learn a lot about digital porn."

Overnight

(NINE)

Since Kristof was relatively new to New York and the East Coast, he wanted to rent a car for a little getaway. So, he told me that he was going to be picking me up for a surprise overnight trip. It would be our first one! The only thing he had told me was to dress casually and to pack for only one night.

All week, I had been bugging him, trying to figure out where he was planning to take me. I knew it couldn't be somewhere too far since he had planned for us to leave on Saturday evening and then to return on Sunday. Knowing that Kristof was somewhat of a history buff, I asked him if we were going to Philadelphia, or upstate somewhere, or maybe to the Jersey Shore? But no, he wouldn't budge. He remained tight-lipped and wouldn't even give me a single hint.

When the day finally arrived, Kristof texted me that he was downstairs waiting for me. I grabbed my overnight bag and went downstairs. As soon as I walked out the lobby of my building and out to the sidewalk, Kristof got out of the car and greeted me with a kiss. Then, he said, "Have you figured out yet what I have planned for you?"

"No, the suspense has been killing me."

Noticing my overnight bag, Kristof reached out his hand to take it from me and said, "Let me get that for you. The door's open."

I walked over to the passenger side of the car and got in as Kristof put my bag in the trunk. Kristof was always doing little things like this, pulling out a chair for me, and holding the door open for me.

As I watched him get into the driver's seat and start driving, I smiled. I liked what I saw. Kristof looked over at me and said, "What's that smug look on your face about?"

"Oh nothing," I paused. "I think I could get used to this, having you drive me around."

"It's my pleasure," Kristof said as he reached for my hand.

"I feel like this is kind of a milestone in a relationship, us going on an overnight trip."

"Yes, I suppose you're right, but it's not like we haven't had any overnight dates yet," Kristof said.

"Yes, and you have always been a perfect gentleman."

"And this will be no different," Kristof said as we approached the entrance to the Holland Tunnel. "We will just be in a different state."

"I see, but when you travel with someone or spend twenty-four hours straight with them, you learn a lot about them and see if you are compatible. I once went to London with my friend Lila, and we were going to stay at her brother's flat while he was away on holiday. I was really excited and after we arrived, I started making all these plans of what I wanted to see and do, but Lila just wanted to take a nap to get over her jet lag. She hadn't been able to sleep on the plane ride over."

"I see, so then what?" Kristof asked without taking his eyes off the road.

"Well, we only had one key between the two of us, and Lila didn't want to give it to me so I just stayed in and looked over my guidebook planning what to do for the rest of our trip while she napped. But after a few days, it started becoming an issue because we were always trying to find some middle ground on what to do together or we'd have to coordinate a time to meet back at the flat. Eventually, I ended up just renting a room at an inn nearby for the last few days, so that I could enjoy my vacation and come and go as I pleased without having to get clearance from a gatekeeper. That's when I realized, you really get to know someone, when you travel together and are around that person twenty-four/seven. Lila and I had such different energy levels and interests. I like to be on the go and to explore, but she just wanted to take it easy."

"Well, you don't have to worry about that. This trip is about us. The two of us to have some time together," Kristof said reassuring me as he reached over and squeezed my hand softly.

After nearly an hour and a half of driving, I started to see signs for Jenny Jump State Park. I had a pretty good guess of what Kristof had planned, but just to make sure asked him, "Are you taking me to the observatory at Jenny Jump?"

"Yes, for some stargazing. I know that you've been fascinated with astronomy since childhood and it's kind of hard to do that in Manhattan. So, I looked into where the closest place to the city to do that would be."

"Thank you! This is amazing. It's so sweet of you," I said as I leaned over to kiss Kristof on the cheek.

"And that's not all, there are supposed to be meteor showers this weekend."

"Wow! I can't wait!"

The Jenny Jump Park turned out to be one of the darkest places on earth that I've ever been. Kristof had prepared some flashlights and glow sticks for us to navigate the darkness. You'd think that being in a place like this would make you feel as if you were in the middle of nowhere, but as I looked at the wondrous, stardust filled sky, I didn't feel alone or isolated at all. I did feel like a little speck in the cosmos, which is vast beyond our comprehension, and that was humbling. The sky looked as if it had been sprinkled with fairy dust. Since there was a meteor shower, we saw quite a few shooting stars streaking across the sky, every few minutes or so. Sharing the experience with Kristof was magical.

In the midst of all this excitement, Kristof said, "I think this deserves a toast." He reached into the duffle bag he'd been carrying, pulled out two plastic cups from it, quietly popped open a bottle of champagne, and poured some into a cup for me and then himself. "Nine I don't know if you realize this, but it's been about two months since we met. And I can't imagine not having you in my life. I love you and really do want to see where things are going with us. So, I've been thinking, maybe we should join The Journey's engaged couples' group together. Even though we're not engaged yet, I think that this is the right time for us to do this and move forward."

I couldn't believe what I heard him saying. I had been expecting the unexpected but nothing like this. "Oh Kristof. This night has been so full of surprises. I love you too, and I think it's a great idea that we join the engaged couples' group together." At that moment I felt so blessed. We kissed under the star-filled sky, as shooting stars flew by overhead. It was as if Mother Nature was staging a fireworks show for us.

As we drove to our lodging, Kristof said, "Now I know you are used to luxury accommodations, but I thought it would be good to really make this memorable by staying overnight in the park. But the options here are limited."

"No problem, it is a state park after all," I said in response.

When I entered the room, I saw that it had a bunk bed, so I said to him, "I guess this is the moment of truth and we'll see who's going to be on the top and who's going to be on the bottom of this relationship."

"All of the rooms are like this, but how about we share the top bunk?" Kristof suggested.

"Well, if we are going to share, wouldn't it just be easier to be on the bottom?" I asked.

"Top or bottom, it really doesn't matter to me as long as we are together."

Later, we snuggled together, as we had many times before, with Kristof in a T-shirt and shorts, and me in a pajama set. We settled on sleeping on the bottom bunk by the way. It was just easier. Feeling safe and secure in Kristof's embrace, I looked out the window at the star-filled sky. As I listened to the sound of crickets chirping, I thought to myself that this was definitely one of the most romantic nights of my life.

The next morning I thought about what Kristof had said about taking the next step in our relationship and I realized that I had something to ask him before we went down this path together. While we were at breakfast having coffee and waiting for our orders to arrive, I said to him, "I'm really happy that we are going to be in the engaged couples' group together, but now I have something to ask you."

"This sounds serious. Now, I'm in suspense," Kristof said.

"Well, my parents live in the Washington, D.C. area and I usually go there to visit them, but this next weekend they are coming to New York and I have told them about you. My parents have said that they want to meet you, and I think that now, especially, you should definitely all meet."

"Yes, that would seem like the next logical step, but from what you've told me, your father is a General in the Air Force and very protective of you. Should I be scared?"

"Well, let's just say that the last time I introduced him to one of my former boyfriends Paul, my Dad kind of grilled him. My Dad does have a real commanding presence and he can be intimidating. That's just the way he is."

"Next month, my older sister Ann is going to be in town for a visit, so you can meet her. She is also very protective of me, so we will see whether both of us will survive the family grilling."

"We've only been pseudo-engaged for one night and we already have in-law issues. Lord, help us!" I said laughing.

"I hope they cover how to handle in-laws in the engaged couples' group."

We both had a laugh about it as we continued the discussion in the car ride home. After I got back home, I went to The Journey's website to find out when the engaged couples' group started and what book we'd be reading together. Then, I searched for the book on Amazon. As I looked through the table of contents, I was relieved to see that it had a big section on in-laws. Several hours later Kristof texted me:

> I looked it up and the group meets on Wednesdays at 7 P.M. Do you want me to register both of us? Speak now or forever hold your peace :-)

I wrote back:

> Thanks. That works for me. I looked up the book and there is a chapter about in-laws. By the way, the 'speak now or forever hold your peace' applies to anyone who has any reason to object. So, let's make sure we nip that in the bud where our potential in-laws are concerned. :-D

I finally felt like my love life was going in the right direction.

The Elusive Double Date

(MONTOYA)

I always try to make friends with at least one neighbor in any apartment building that I live in and I really lucked out this time. The day I moved into my Upper East Side apartment, I met Mandy. She was very cute with a mischievous smile and I liked her immediately. I asked her how she liked living in the building.

Then, I found out she lived on my floor, but she wasn't single. When I met her husband Mike, I liked him also. Mike was Danish and an architect. Mandy was from Singapore and a scientist working on finding a cure for cancer. For whatever reason, it seemed like their pairing was very natural. Some things just seem to go together, like peanut butter and jelly, peas and carrots, or wine and cheese.

As for myself, I must admit ever since I had fallen for Mai in London, I have always been partial to Asian women. But I have also definitely had a sampling of many different types of women other than Asian—blonde, brunette, redhead, Black, Latina, Indian— you name it.

The first time I went out for drinks with Mandy and Mike, I liked their playful banter. Mike kept going on and on about how Mandy had forgotten his birthday. Mandy would just roll her eyes sweetly as if to make fun of Mike and say he was being a baby. I kept trying to do a double date with the two of them. I knew it would be fun to go out to dinner with the two of them, and I knew that they'd be able to share their frank impressions of whomever it was I was dating. But that was easier said than done. Trying to arrange four different people's busy schedules in New York City for a sit down dinner is pretty hard to do.

Add to this the fact that I go through my relationships faster than women flash their tits for beads at Mardi Gras. None of my relationships so far had lasted long enough to go on this elusive double date. The one exception was Evelyn. This on-again, off-again relationship did last a long time, actually too long. And, curiously, every time I arranged a double date with Mandy and Mike, somehow Evelyn and I had a fight or argument. So, dinner after dinner, it was just Mike, Mandy, and me.

When I arranged my first double date with Joy, I expected somehow, some way that Joy and I would have a fight or break-up. It seemed like getting to the double date was a test of whether the relationship had any staying power and any legs to stand on. So, when Joy didn't cancel or postpone, I thought, so far so good. Finally, when the day came and Joy showed up at Brasserie Julien, right on time no less, Mandy and Mike looked at me in amazement and I couldn't wipe off the smile that I had on my face all night.

"Maybe you should buy a lottery ticket today," Mandy said alluding to this change in my fortune, relationship-wise, that is.

I think it was at that double date that I fell in love with Joy. It must have registered in my face as I was listening to Mandy and Joy compare notes on where they both liked to shop and eat in Singapore. Joy must have noticed me staring at her, because she stopped in mid-sentence and asked, "Montoya, why that look?"

"Nothing, just happy you are here," I replied. But what I was thinking was that Montoya and Joy went together as well as gin and tonic or fish and chips. A new natural pairing had been made.

YEAR III

SUMMER

The Good, The Bad and The Tantric
(LUANA)

Summers in New York City are literally the good, the bad and the ugly. For me, the good would be the men jogging through Central Park, toned and shirtless. For men, it would be women wearing form-fitting shorts or short skirts with barely-there tops, or skimpy little dresses. The best thing about summers in the Big Apple is the hot and steamy sex. With all this exposed skin, everywhere you look, everyone seems to go into heat.

Now, that doesn't mean that everyone is sniffing each other's butts in the park, but it does create a lot of post-hookup laundry bills in order to clean up all that sweating between the sheets. Then, there's the bad part of Manhattan summers, the non-air conditioned subway stations where everyone is sweating profusely. It wouldn't be so bad if everyone in the subway looked like a supermodel. Manhattan is a paradox with some of the most beautiful people in the world and others who look like they've escaped from a circus sideshow.

I had met Gavino at a friend's party and he was no freak show. He was a tall former model who was now running his family's restaurant business in Malta. He was visiting New York for a week, and it was his last night in the city. So, after we met, we decided to go dancing together; and what a dancer he was. As Gavino and I danced, it was as if we moved as one.

When the music slowed down, our dancing and conversation got hot and heavy. Without even saying anything, I could tell that

Gavino knew what he was doing by the way he moved his body. I wanted him and then Gavino asked if I had ever been with someone who knew how to practice tantric sex, which meant that he could control when he had his orgasm. I started making out with him right on the dance floor and invited him back to my place basically giving him the green light to sleep with me.

We couldn't get to my apartment soon enough. The first time I came was when he went down on me. The second time I screamed because Gavino was really that good in bed. He was in a class all by himself. Gavino seemed to enjoy making me go crazy. He didn't need to stop or rest. I felt like the New York Marathon had begun early for me this year—in my bedroom.

With each orgasm, I screamed louder and louder. Then, I yelled out, *"Ai, me deus do ceu!"*

Gavino looked a little puzzled and said, "Are you cursing me out or do you want me to keep going?"

"No, I said 'Oh my God!' in Portuguese. Don't you dare stop!"

The fourth time I came was as he was doing me doggy style and slapping my butt. The fifth was me on top of him while he was pinching my nipples with both of his hands. I swear this guy could be a classical pianist, what hands! He was literally pounding my brains out. I think I am pretty good with numbers, but I lost count of how many times I came. I was so exhausted that I couldn't think clearly any longer.

Finally, with my mind in a haze, I remembered him saying he was getting tired and finally he came. I was so weak and exhausted that I just fell into a deep sleep. I woke up terribly late for work at 3 P.M. and I realized that Gavino had already left. Every muscle in my body felt sore as I tried to get out of bed. I was still tingling from the marathon that Gavino had put me through. Then, I saw a note on my nightstand. It read:

Luana,

Great spending time with you. That was a good workout… just a little under six hours long. I stopped when you lost your voice. I don't know how many times you came. My body is very relaxed… now, I will get a good sleep on the flight back to Malta.

It was fun,

Gavino

How could that be possible? Had I really lost my voice? I tried to speak and not a sound came out. I couldn't believe it. I had screamed so many times that for the first time in my life, I had laryngitis—from sex. I emailed my boss and wrote that I was sorry but I had woken up with laryngitis and a terrible flu. I told him that I would be out for a few days, and would work from home.

In the heat of passion during my hot and steamy night with Gavino, I never even got his last name. Unbelievable! The screw of the century and I had no way to reach him.

In This Life and the Next

(FRANK)

Leah was lying in her bed with me. We were caressing each other's bodies after having just made love. Her daughter, Shanti, was in the other room asleep, so we talked quietly keeping our voices down.

"Do you think that we knew each other in a previous life?" Leah asked.

"Another life? You believe in reincarnation?" I responded.

"Of course, I haven't talked to you much about my spiritual beliefs, but my entire family is Hindu."

"Well, I was raised Catholic, but I haven't been to church in years, so I guess you can say I am a lapsed Catholic or maybe even an agnostic. But really, maybe I might even be an atheist. When I read the newspaper and see all the evil in the world, it makes me wonder, where is God?"

"Well, when it comes to evil, I really do believe in karma. To me, karma makes a lot of sense," Leah shared.

"Not sure if I believe in karma, but I do believe in 'Instant Karma' as John Lennon sang about. I believe that what goes around comes around."

"So, do you believe we were a couple in a previous life?" Leah asked again.

"I am not sure. Maybe."

"I think we were a couple. I think I know you. Really know you. Like in multiple lifetimes."

"Wow. That is deep. A couple as in married?"

"Yes. When I make love to you, it feels so familiar—like we have done it thousands of times."

In the subdued light of Leah's bedroom, I looked into Leah's eyes for a long time.

"What?" Leah asked.

I then said, "I have an idea. Shanti is on vacation from school all summer. I run my own business, so I can take off whenever I feel like it. You like the water, so let me take both of you on several long weekend trips to the Caribbean. It will give us a chance to all get to know each other better."

"That would be great," she said excitedly.

I knew Leah had an affinity for water. The city she grew up in, Goa, was right by the ocean. Now in New York, she lived near Riverside Park with a good view of the Hudson River. Leah and I planned three weekend getaways during the summer, one for June, one for July, and one for August.

Our first destination was St. Maarten as the Dutch call it, or Saint-Martin, as the French dub it. The island is divided into the side owned by France and the side owned by the Netherlands. Both sides either have topless beaches or allow you to be topless, but the French side has the only officially nude beach. While Shanti went on a glass-bottom boat excursion for kids organized by the hotel, Leah and I went to the nude beach on the French side. Leah had on a one-piece swimsuit, but I peeled off my swimsuit to let everyone on the beach get to know me better.

Our next weekend trip was to Bermuda, the land of pink beaches. It had less nightlife than the other Caribbean islands and was populated by the descendants of real pirates. Despite this, it was a very calm and serene place. On the first day at the beach, Leah put some pink sand in an empty water bottle to bring back with her and Shanti made a pink sand castle.

On our last trip in August, we went to the Atlantis resort in the Bahamas, an all-inclusive resort. It had a lagoon surrounding the hotel, which was actually an aquarium where you could swim with the fish. But unlike the movie, *The Godfather*, the plan was not to die when you "swam with the fishes." There were large manta rays and Leah was ecstatic about swimming with them. I watched and took photos of Shanti and Leah in the aquarium lagoon since I had never learned how to swim. When both of them emerged from the aquarium lagoon, they were giddy from the experience. Afterward, Shanti slid down the giant water slide at the aquarium. For the adventurous, the hotel even had a shark tank.

After dinner, when Shanti was asleep in the adjoining room, Leah said, "I want to get into the shark tank."

I responded, "Well that is kind of scary, but I know you love the water. That would be a great experience for you. Whatever floats your boat."

"I want you to join me," she said hesitantly.

"Are you crazy?" I said laughing. "You know I don't know how to swim. I thought we were getting along great as a couple. But I think if my girlfriend wants me to drown to my death that shows there is a problem with the relationship."

"Wow! That is the first time you called me 'your girlfriend.' "

"Well, uh, yes you are definitely my girlfriend... but not sure how long that is going to last with me drowning or maybe being eaten by sharks. Sharks!" I repeated in disbelief.

Leah responded, "It is totally safe. They give you one of those helmets and an oxygen tank attached to the helmet. You climb down a ladder and walk, not swim, walk on the bottom of the tank."

"You do realize I can't swim?"

"Of course, but it is perfectly safe, I read all about it. There are three men with you as you climb down the ladder and they stay with you in the shark tank."

"And if one of the sharks decides to bite my dick off, are they going to protect me? Really?"

"It is safe. Trust me," Leah reassured me.

The next day, I stripped down to my swimming trunks and Leah to her one-piece swimsuit before we each put on our wetsuits. Shanti was busy elsewhere at a program for children.

"Are you okay Frank? You seem to be sweating up a storm," Leah said focusing her attention on me with a look of concern.

"Yeah, this wetsuit makes me feel like I'm in a sauna," I replied.

"Are you sure it's not nerves? Trust me, I wouldn't bring you down there if I thought the shark was going to try to bite your dick off," Leah said laughing.

We waited for one group to exit the tank before going down along with another couple. After receiving instructions from one of the guides, Leah descended the stairs about 30 feet into the shark tank. I followed right behind her. The sharks swam about 10 feet above us in the tank. I had the helmet on which had water in it up to my chin. I was trying very hard to keep my head level because if you looked down, up, or sideways, the water came up into my nostrils.

One of the guides handed me a sea urchin and gave Leah a starfish and motioned for us to hold them up and pose for a photo. We walked around the bottom of the tank holding each other's hand. There was a strong underwater current that bumped against us making it hard for us to keep our balance. I held onto Leah's hand for dear life the entire time. After about fifteen minutes, it was time to surface.

While taking off my wetsuit, I proclaimed, "That was the most romantic thing I have ever done."

"Really? You were holding my hand really tight down there," Leah replied.

"Yes, I was scared for my life and yet I was holding your hand the entire time. Then, I started to feel calm and I felt a little of that past life thing that you were talking about."

After dinner at the resort, Leah took Shanti back up to the room and tucked her into bed. Through the hotel's front desk, she had gotten in touch with a babysitter who she had met and judged trustworthy enough to look after Shanti for the night. Once Leah had given the babysitter instructions, she and I went to get a drink at one of the bars at the resort.

At the bar, I drank a glass of white wine and stared at Leah.

"What? You seem to be doing a lot of this blank staring lately," Leah remarked. "The glassy-eyed look doesn't make you look good," she said joshing me.

"I love you," I said and then kissed Leah on the lips.

This was the first time I had expressed my feelings so directly to her. Leah paused and after a few moments she replied, "I love you too, Frank! So much!"

And then I asked her, "If—it is just an if—if we were thinking of really being serious, would you expect me to convert to Hinduism?"

"It means a great deal to my family and, I guess to me also."

"What would that involve?"

"Well, to start with, I try to read the Bhagavad Gita at least once a week. I know that I should read it more often. It's also called the Gita, and it contains some of the most sacred Hindu scriptures."

"Okay, can you get me an abridged translation? I'd better see what I am getting myself into," I said making a joke.

That evening, again in each other's arms in bed, Leah kissed me passionately. "I think you and I are soul mates. I love you in this life and the next," Leah said between kisses.

"I think you might make a believer out of me," I said. "I love you too."

Don't Forget the Girlfriend

(MONTOYA)

I never thought I would enjoy holding hands as much as I do with Joy. Everywhere we go, when we become separated in a crowd, I would automatically reach back my hand, extending it in search of her hand. It gave me a real sense of comfort, holding her hand. She loved to do little things for me like fix me a cup of tea or rub my shoulders. As for myself, I called her every day. This is something that every guy knows you need to do to keep a girlfriend, but with Joy, I actually looked forward to talking to her daily.

Since I was now in a serious relationship, I had stopped being as social as I used to be. Friends would text me or call me and ask what happened. Why did my invites stop? I repeatedly explained that I was entering a new phase in my life and that I needed to give Joy quality time. With all the people I knew in New York, there were always plenty of events to go to such as birthday parties, networking socials, gallery openings, and others. And now, wherever I went, Joy was my constant companion.

Frank was also in a serious relationship and we decided to make sure that our friendship wouldn't suffer now that we were both in new relationships. So, we would get together every now and then for a drink to catch up. I would also make sure that I got together with Nine, Luana, and Tara for some one-on-one time. I am not one of those who will give up close friends once I'm in a relationship.

But soon a problem that I hadn't anticipated surfaced. Joy had met every ex-girlfriend who I was friends with, who lived in New

York. But there were still some exes who I kept in touch with who didn't live in New York.

One of them was Madison. She now lived in Dubai, and I hadn't seen her in years. She was also married now, so when she told me she'd be in town on a visit, I didn't see anything wrong with getting together with her just to catch up. I had planned to meet her at 6:30 in the evening before Joy and I were going to go see a movie at 9:30 that night. I told Joy I would be done with my dinner with Madison by 9 P.M.

Madison had grown up an atheist and during dinner, we started talking about God. We had never talked about God or religion, and I excitedly shared my newly found recommitment to God with her. We talked about her feelings and beliefs about church, Christians, and God. Since Madison was in town for a conference for the entire week, she accepted my invitation to The Journey Church for the coming Sunday night. And she also agreed to come to the growth group that Joy and I were in.

When I finally checked my watch, I was shocked to see that it was already 10 P.M. I couldn't believe it. I had become so engrossed in our conversation about spirituality that I had totally forgotten about Joy. I checked my text messages. There were several from Joy. I immediately paid the bill and said goodbye to Madison. Then, I called Joy who told me she was back at home.

I got in a cab and when I arrived at her block, I stopped to buy a dozen roses for her. I buzzed Joy's apartment and held up the dozen roses as a peace offering. I knew that she could see me through her intercom camera. Joy let me in and when I got upstairs and she opened the door, I went to try to kiss her, but she turned her head to the side.

"I am so so sorry for this. I was with my friend Madison and we just lost track of the time," I said.

"But you knew we were going to the movie at 9:30. How could you just forget me?"

"Madison is an atheist and we started taking about religion and faith. We had never talked about this before. I just totally lost track of time. Both of us checked our watches and couldn't believe that we had talked for three hours. The time just zoomed by. I am very sorry that we missed the movie."

"It's not about the movie. You were with another woman and you totally forgot that I existed. That is the problem. I waited for an hour for you," Joy said angrily.

"I know. I know. I am really sorry. I felt like I was doing God's will. I am not using that as an excuse. It's just that I haven't seen Madison for years and this is the first time that she opened up regarding spirituality. I talked to her about The Bible, Jesus, church, everything. I was so excited and enthusiastic, I totally lost track of time. I am really sorry," I responded.

"Who is this Madison anyway? Why haven't you seen her for years?"

"She is an ex who is now married and lives in Dubai," I responded.

"An ex?" Joy said with an angry look on her face.

"A married ex. Emphasis on the word married."

"Really? You were with an attractive woman, who also happens to be your ex for three hours, you totally forgot about your girl-friend, and now you use God as an excuse?"

"Joy, it is the truth. Actually, I was doing a really good thing. She is coming to The Journey this Sunday, so you'll get to meet her. This is a big deal for her because she has never been to church before. Honestly, all we did was talk about faith."

"That may be the case, but you totally forgot me. If you don't mind, I am tired and need to be by myself right now."

I left Joy's apartment feeling like a dolt. How could I just forget her? But seriously, there is no instruction manual for having a relationship. There really isn't. You have to learn that women want you to call them every day. You have to figure out what a woman's little subtle cues mean and many times they expect you to have psychic or telepathic ability in understanding them.

And by the way, having a girlfriend does take up a lot of your time. They need both quality time and quantity time. They never want you to say anything good about your ex-girlfriends. They like it when you do little thoughtful acts, whisper sweet little nothings in their ear, and then listen when they vent about their day. I am much more sensitive than the average guy, and even though I have a million women friends, I don't really understand women all the time. So what chance does the average guy have?

Madison wasn't able to make it to the Sunday evening service that Joy and I usually attended, so I went with her in the morning. At the evening service, Joy was quieter than usual and was still kind of giving me the cold shoulder. In the past with Evelyn, we were always butting heads on something, but with Joy it was different. I never knew where I stood with Evelyn; the rules seemed to change all the time. With Joy there were no games. I knew that as a Christian, Joy at least would eventually forgive me.

A week later, Joy called me to tell me about a conversation she had. "Hi Montoya, I've been thinking about our last argument and decided to ask my friends Linda and David, who are a couple, for some advice. They also go to The Journey and lead a couples' growth group," Joy explained.

"Okay. So, what did they say?"

"Linda said that David has done the same thing as you and had forgotten her on a few occasions. She made me realize that sometimes it happens and that we are all human."

"See, I'm not that bad after all," I said feeling relieved that our argument was finally over.

"She even said that although you were having dinner with an ex, I should look at your intentions. You were talking to her about God, after all."

"So, am I out of the doghouse?"

"Yes, but I am making sure you are on a short leash," Joy said and I could tell that she was joking and had lightened up.

I was glad that she was back to showing her playful side again. I learned that rule number one in having a girlfriend is don't forget that you have one. Don't forget to introduce her as your girlfriend to your friends when you're at an event. Don't forget to include her in conversations if she's at an event where she doesn't know anybody. Don't forget her birthday. Don't forget your anniversary. And above all, don't forget that she doesn't forget.

Totally Resistible

(ROXANNE and Tara)

I missed being a reporter out in the field and decided that being a news anchor and in Boston didn't suit me. I had missed the energy of New York. Now that I had returned, the first order of business was to get back into the Manhattan social scene. So, I called up my favorite wing woman, Tara.

"Hi Tara, I can't believe that you will be leaving the country soon, now that I just moved back to New York. We have to get together."

"Yes, I've missed you! My other half, my wing woman," Tara replied. "I'm only going for a couple of weeks. I'll be back before you know it."

We decided to go to a networking event at a trendy little bar in Chelsea. As I stood by the bar waiting for my drink to be prepared, I felt someone looking at me. I looked over my shoulder and recognized him right away. It was Leonard, a stocky Midwestern guy. He had noticed me too apparently and was walking toward me. This guy really has some balls, I thought to myself.

"You look as lovely as ever. I can't believe that I never had you. It's still not too late," Leonard said winking as he looked me up and down.

"You are unbelievable. It didn't happen then and it's not going to happen now. I think you'd better try to find someone else more willing," I said promptly walking away.

"What was that all about?" Tara asked. Apparently she had seen the exchange and the way Leonard had looked me up and down.

"Yeah, well not only did he just proposition me, but there's a story there. I actually first met him a few years ago."

"Oh really? So, what's the story?" Tara asked.

"I met him during one of my runs in the park," I said.

"Somehow, that doesn't surprise me. You can meet men anywhere!"

"Yeah, I used to always bump into him during my runs in the park. Actually, when I'm on my runs, I'm usually pretty focused and not really looking to socialize with anyone. He would smile and say hi, and after we bumped into each other a few times, he'd strike up a conversation. He was just really goofy. After a while, we'd sometimes run together. I had the impression that he was interested because he had been dropping hints and finally after a few weeks of this he asked me out."

"Oh. So, what did you do on your first date?"

"Well, sometimes when we ran around the park, we'd run by that area where there are all these roller skaters and roller bladers dancing around in a big loop to some dance music," I continued.

"Oh totally. They are like a permanent fixture in the park. It's like a mini-block party. They always look like they are having so much fun. I think they have been around so long that they are even organized into some sort of club or association."

"Right. So, whenever we'd run by there, he'd say that maybe we should join them."

"Oooo, that does sound like fun. Though, I'd be a bit intimidated to skate around that crowd, I can rollerblade just fine, but I don't think that I could keep up with them or move the way they do. I'd probably lose my balance if I tried to shake my bootie to the music while trying to rollerblade. Those people seriously get down and dance," Tara said.

"He invited me to spend the afternoon at the roller skating/roller-blading mini-block party at Prospect Park in Brooklyn. And since he lived nearby, he offered to cook dinner for me afterward. It seemed like a fun idea, so I said okay, but only dinner and nothing else."

"Ha ha right. Don't let him get the wrong idea."

"Yeah, and it was a lot of fun. As a kid I used to love to roller skate at the local rink. Afterward, he made this wonderful stir fry. I had a lot of fun with him. He just knew how to make me laugh. We shared a bottle of wine, and it was getting late. I said something about heading home, but he said, 'Why are you leaving, what are you afraid of? Afraid you won't be able to resist me if you stay?'"

"I just laughed at him and said, 'No, of course, I'm not afraid of you.' So, he said, 'Just stay. I'll let you choose, do you want to sleep in the bed with me or on the sofa?' Frankly, I really felt exhausted, didn't want to bother calling for a car, and was sleepy from roller blading and the wine. He seemed harmless, so I said I'd be fine on the sofa. So, he gave me some sheets, and laid them out on the sofa for me. Then, he went back into his bedroom."

"Oh that's good," said Tara.

"But there's more. After he went into his room, he turned on some music, and just as I realized that it was Marvin Gaye's 'Let's Get It On,' he appeared in the living room, totally butt naked, and said, 'Come on baby, are you sure you don't want to try any of this?' I just looked at him up and down and said, 'Sorry honey, I don't think you quite meet my minimum requirements.'"

"Seriously?! He did that? You definitely put him in his place."

"So, he said, 'Are you sure you don't want to take a ride on this love machine? It's not size that matters. Like they say, what really matters is the motion of the ocean.' And to that I said, 'I do have my standards and that ain't going to cut it.'"

"Oh wow, and so then what did he do?" Tara's eyes widened.

"So he said, 'Damn Roxanne! Okay, I get it. You have your standards. I got it. I can respect that. No problem.' And he went back into his room."

"Oh wow, so did he really leave you alone?"

"Yup, he didn't bother me for the rest of the night."

"And it wasn't awkward the morning after?"

"Well, I had slept in my clothes, so I just woke up and slipped out without waking him up, leaving a note or saying goodbye."

"So, did you ever bump into him again after that?"

"Well, I started running along another route."

Tara looked over to Leonard who was on the other side of the bar, talking to several men and looking directly at me. "Do you think he is telling those guys that he slept with you?" she asked.

"At this point, I could care less. He can say whatever he wants to make himself look good to his friends," I replied.

"I'm not sure I am as brave as you are. I don't think I would sleep over at a guy's apartment I wasn't dating unless he was a good friend like Frank or Montoya. If I was in the same situation, I would be apprehensive of the man not getting the subtle hint or in your case the blunt truth that you weren't interested."

"You'd think that choosing the sofa would be the most unsubtle of hints! When guys offer the bed or the sofa, it is like sex roulette with 50/50 odds. Most men are willing to play the odds that half the women will choose the bed. And then when a woman doesn't choose the bed, it's still open to interpretation for a lot of men. You just never know in the game of love. People can be unpredictable and self-contradictory," Roxanne declared.

Saying I Do

(MONTOYA and Nine)

Joy and I had just finished dinner in my apartment. But this was not just any meal; it was Joy's birthday. I consider myself a gentleman and have bought women flowers, candy, and jewelry, as well as paid for exotic vacations together. However, I would never and have never cooked a woman dinner. I hate cooking. Not just a little bit, I mean I really hate it. It seems like a total waste of time when there are so many great takeout places and restaurants in New York. I've always enjoyed learning about the latest restaurants on Grub Hub or from New York Magazine or Time Out New York. So, why cook?

But for some women, a man cooking dinner for them was better than going down on them. I hate cooking so much that I've always said that if I ever cook a dinner for a girlfriend, it meant I was thinking of proposing marriage. Joy had overheard me say this to Nine. So, when I offered to cook her dinner, she initially raised an eyebrow, giving me the same look that Spock often had on his face on Star Trek. I downplayed it by saying that it was just a gesture of love on my part to cook her dinner, but she and I both knew that it meant much more. After dinner, we sat on the couch and relaxed.

"Montoya, I need to talk to you about something serious. We seem like a great match. But…"

"But what?"

"But you've never been baptized."

"I have been going to The Journey for several months now and I even started reading The Bible every day. Isn't that enough?"

"Baptism is different. It is a public acknowledgment of your faith."

"A public acknowledgment? I get it. It's similar to getting married being a public acknowledgment. You think I can't commit. That you might be wasting your time with me?"

"Maybe. After all, how many women have you dated in New York?" she said bemused.

Joy had been engaged previously and came close to marriage. But he was not a Christian, and they had started dating prior to her becoming Christian and a member of The Journey. When the date of the wedding came closer, Joy felt more and more uneasy about the prospect of being married to someone who didn't share her new faith. So, she reluctantly and very sadly broke off the engagement. I knew that this was hard for her and it showed how important it was to her that the man in her life would also have a commitment to Christ.

Our relationship had hit a crossroads. I knew what Joy needed for our relationship to move forward. So, I had a decision to make.

Afterward, I thought about what Joy was looking for. But I also thought about why it was that I was so attracted to Joy. She was smart, pretty, and fun to be with, but so were many other women who I have dated. So, what was it about her? Finally, I came to the conclusion that she inspired me to be a better person and more importantly, a better Christian.

Yet, how could I get her to think I was a serious marriage candidate when I couldn't commit publicly to God? What was preventing me from being baptized now? I really didn't have any good reasons not to be baptized as an adult. I had come full circle.

Originally raised in a devout Christian family, I was now back in a personal relationship with Jesus. But this time, it wasn't just because of my family. God had reached out to me, and I felt that he was now as real to me as he was to Joy, Nine, or my Mum. But baptism seemed as serious as a marriage commitment. The Journey had baptisms every three months and the upcoming one was the largest one of the year. It was a beach baptism, which would be done at Jones Beach on Long Island. I decided that I would make my relationship to Jesus official, not only for Joy's sake, but for myself.

When I signed up and told Joy about my decision, she was thrilled and said she would come with me. I told Nine, and she and Kristof also wanted to come along. As the four of us rode on the Long Island railroad, I realized how things had changed for both Nine and me, and it was as if I had come to some kind of a turning point. Then, as we got on the bus to the beach, I started to feel butterflies in my stomach. I was nervous, but couldn't understand why. Was it possible? Was I going to get cold feet?

At the beach, about two hundred people from The Journey assembled. As I looked around, I noticed that many of the women from The Journey were in bikinis, as were Joy and Nine. Now, this isn't something that you would normally expect to see at a baptism. Okay, so this isn't that bad, I thought. Bikinis I can handle.

Kerrick led the group in prayer and told those of us being baptized that this was a big step in our lives. No kidding! I felt those butterflies back in my stomach again. Those of us being baptized were asked to form a line, and then one-by-one each of us was to head out to the water to be dunked by Kerrick and the other pastors. Nelson Searcy, who is the lead pastor of The Journey Church, had also come for this event. He came over and talked to me a bit seeing that I looked very nervous.

"Don't worry. We are all here to support you," Nelson reassured me.

"This is just a big step for me."

"I will be praying for you. You will be fine," Nelson responded.

Joy kissed me on the lips, then Nine gave me a kiss on my cheek, and Kristof gave me a pat on the back, as they left me so I could go stand in the Baptism line. They took out their cameras, ready to capture the moment. Waiting in that line seemed like an eternity, although it was just ten minutes. Finally, when it was my turn, I waded out to where the pastors were.

"Montoya, do you accept Jesus Christ as your Lord and Savior?" Kerrick asked.

"I do." My God, I thought. This is like marriage. I just said "I do."

"Then, in the name of the Father, the Son, and the Holy Spirit. I baptize you," Kerrick said as he dunked my entire body in the ocean and in another swift movement brought me back up.

"Buried with Christ and raised to new life in him," Kerrick announced.

I was dripping with water as Kerrick and the other pastors gave me a hug. I waded back to the beach to be greeted by Joy and Nine. Nine and Kristof each gave me a hug but Joy started to French kiss me right there on the beach.

"I feel like I am married to God now," I said to Joy as an inside joke.

But for Joy, I think that public acknowledgment to God was as if I had just taken a step closer to marriage. She was glowing with a smile that wouldn't go away. On the trip back to Manhattan, I could tell that Joy felt that God had washed away not just my sins, but also any fears of commitment.

Later, when we were in private, Joy playfully said to me, "Okay, so now I know that you are able to make a commitment."

Rivers to Cross

(TARA)

It had been an intense week. So much had happened since I had arrived in Cambodia. I had come as a Nomi Network volunteer to actually see the work that they did firsthand. When I told my parents and close friends that I'd decided to go on this trip, they all knew how important it was for me on many personal levels.

On the first day of my arrival in Phnom Penh, I walked into the breakfast orientation meeting and scanned the room for a few familiar faces. I immediately saw Diana, who was usually one of the tallest Asian women in a room. She and her Nomi Network co-founders, Alissa Moore and Supei Liu, were all enthusiastically greeting volunteers before the meeting got underway. I had met all three women in New York. They were the only three familiar faces in the room.

Feeling like a kid on the first day of school, I was surprised to hear someone calling my name. I turned around and saw that it was Terence. Unbelievable! He looked just as I'd remembered. In fact, he looked even more tan, relaxed, and toned. I wondered if he'd been working out more lately. It seemed that the California lifestyle suited him.

"You're here, you made it," he said as if it wasn't a surprise at all that I was there. "I mean, I had no idea you'd be here but whatever it is that brought you here, I'm just glad to see you," he said as he leaned over to give me a kiss on the cheek.

"I'm glad to see you, too. Are you here working on another film?" I asked noticing the camera bag, video camera, and tripod that he was carrying.

"I'm here to shoot more footage to make my short film about the Nomi Network into a full-length documentary."

"That's great!"

Before I could say any more, Terence said, "I've got to go get everything all set up and I'm not sure if we'll be on the same schedule this week, but let's try to catch up toward the end of the week." Then, he turned and walked away leaving me slightly bewildered. I wondered whether he was attached or not. But soon, I was distracted as the orientation meeting started.

The Nomi Network had a very full week of activities scheduled for the volunteers. Over the course of the week I did periodically see Terence with the film crew, usually in some flurry of activity. On the last day of the trip, the Nomi Network hosted a big farewell dinner for everyone involved with the Nomi Network, not just the volunteers. Afterward, all of the volunteers, except me, went off to the airport to catch late night flights home.

Everyone knew that I was staying behind to go to Thailand next. Most people assumed that I was simply going get some extra R and R, but I'd planned to make the trip to Thailand specifically to visit the orphanage where my biological mother had left me. In the midst of all the goodbyes, Terrence learned that I was staying in Phnom Penh an extra night before heading to Bangkok. So, he asked me, "You want to see the real Phnom Penh after this, where the locals hang out?"

"Sure, I definitely don't have to be up early tomorrow," I said.

Once everyone had said their goodbyes and headed to the airport, Terence and I were finally left alone. He suggested that we go for a ride around town on his motorbike. He handed me a helmet and I got on behind him.

"Just lean forward with me and put your hands around my waist for balance," he instructed me.

Sitting behind him was a kind of an intimate position with my legs straddled on the seat behind him; my thighs hugged him from behind as he drove me around the city. We went to a night market where some vendors were still selling trinkets. After that, we went to a local bar to have a drink. Terence was full of suggestions of things to do and places to see in Thailand. He gave me a laundry list of things to do: get a Thai massage, visit the Grand Palace, see the floating markets and the Reclining Buddha at Wat Pho, then, see a traditional Thai dance performance. He even offered to put me in touch with some of his friends there who'd be able to show me around.

Then he took me to the riverfront for a little stroll. That's when I decided to break the charade. "I know that you, as most people, have assumed that I'm going to Thailand as a tourist, but I'm actually going for a very specific purpose, which I haven't told anyone."

"Oh, really. Now, I'm intrigued."

"The reason I'm going there is to visit the orphanage where my birth mother left me and from where my parents adopted me."

"Wow, I had no idea. Are you looking for your birth mother?"

"No, I doubt that I will find her. When I was adopted, the people at the orphanage told my parents that they thought that my mother might have been Cambodian. They thought that she had escaped from the Khmer Rouge regime. Then, later when I was in my teens, I wrote to the orphanage asking if they had any more information on my biological parents. They didn't. My birth mother didn't have any identification or papers on her when she showed up and left me at the orphanage." My mind wandered a bit as I looked out at the river and saw how the lights of the lampposts danced in the waters. "I wonder what rivers my mother had to cross and what risks she must have had to take to get out of Cambodia."

"I see. This is such a huge trip for you Tara, in a lot of ways."

"Yes, my flight from New York was a round trip in and out of Phnom Penh. From what I've read, it's easier to just purchase a one-way ticket from here to Bangkok. Then, when I'm ready, I'll just book another flight back to Phnom Penh in time to fly back to New York. So, tomorrow I need to stop by a local travel agency to book a flight."

"I can definitely take you to a good travel agency tomorrow to get you a ticket for Bangkok."

"Thanks."

"I'm happy to help. Now that you've told me about your mother, let me share something with you," Terence paused and then said, "I never really knew my father."

"Really? Why not? What happened to him?" I asked with curiosity.

"My older brother has some memory of him, I think. Shortly after I was born, our father took off, leaving our mother to take care of us alone in Taiwan. My mother, she was a tough lady. Her brothers and sister had gotten scholarships to study in the U.S. and she was the last one left behind in Taiwan. She was determined to join them in the U.S., so she found a way to immigrate there and join them. She didn't have a graduate degree, like her siblings, but she made the most of what skills and talents she had. She was an excellent seamstress so she used her tailoring skills to work at a dry cleaners. Soon, she had a bunch of loyal customers and a growing list of clients who encouraged her to go into business for herself as a tailor and dressmaker."

As I listened to what Terence said, my thoughts were still on my mother and I added, "I sometimes wonder what happened to my mother. What made her leave me at the orphanage? What would have happened to me if I had been left in Cambodia, and my mother hadn't taken me to Thailand? Or, what if I hadn't gotten adopted? I looked at those girls this week and I wonder if that could have been me. According to the people at the orphanage, my mother did not seem like she was in good health. That's probably another reason that she gave me up," I felt tears welling up in my eyes. I wiped away my tears feeling a bit embarrassed that I had suddenly gotten so emotional.

Terence stopped and looked at me, "Are you okay?"

"Mmm, hmmmm," I mumbled as I nodded.

We continued walking and then Terence broke the silence between us, "When I was younger, I wondered why my father just disappeared. How could he do that and never look back? I mean, what kind of a man does that? As a boy, I wanted to find him. I had so many questions. I suppose I hoped that one day he would come around looking for us and wanting to make up for lost time. But that never happened, of course. I'm not interested in finding him anymore. He probably doesn't want to be found. It sounds like your mother made a difficult decision because she couldn't take care of you. She did what she thought was best for you."

As I listened to Terence, I wasn't sure what would have been worse, knowing that your father had abandoned you, your brother, and mother, or never knowing who your mother was or where you actually came from.

"I guess having a deadbeat dad is a lot worse than having a long lost mom," I said trying to lighten the mood.

"Oh, so my sob story made you feel better? That's good," Terence grinned. "Well, I haven't exactly decided where I'm going from here yet. I had thought of going to Thailand since I have quite a few friends there who I haven't seen in a while. Would you mind having a travel companion? I could help you figure out where the orphanage is and how to get there. But if you want to go there on your own, or if you feel it's something you want to do on your own, I'll understand. Either way, let me know if you want moral support."

Without much hesitation I found myself saying, "Thanks, it might actually be nice to have a travel companion."

"Okay, so we'll go to the travel agency together tomorrow and book our tickets," Terence said, "Let's head back, it's getting late."

He drove me back to my guesthouse, but when we got there, the front gates were locked. I had no idea that they locked the gates after a certain time. This was the latest that I'd gotten in all week.

"Oh no, I'm sorry about this Tara. Do you have a number for the guesthouse that we can call? You can use my phone to call."

I took out my room key, which had a phone number on it.

"Here, use my phone to call and see if someone from the guesthouse picks up," Terence said handing me his phone.

"Thanks," I took his phone and dialed the number. The phone rang a few times and then the line got disconnected. I tried to call a few more times and the same thing happened. "Hmmmm it's odd, I can't seem to get through. It rings a few times and then the phone hangs up," I handed him back his phone.

"Really? That's odd. Well, the inn that I'm staying at is nearby. You can take the bed and I'll order an extra cot or something. I promise I'll be a gentleman."

"No, no don't do that. I'm the one who should be taking the cot," I insisted.

When we got to the room, Terence said, "I insist you take the bed."

By then, the wine that I'd had earlier in the evening had taken effect, making me feel drowsy, so I didn't protest and laid on the bed closing my eyes and said, "Thanks you're the best."

I heard Terence pick up the phone and call for an extra cot. Soon, there was a knock on the door. I heard Terence talking to someone, and then the door closed.

The room felt comfortably air-conditioned. Terence came over and pulled the bed sheets over me. "Goodnight Tara," he whispered.

"Stay, just sleep here with me," I whispered back half asleep. Soon, I was asleep with Terence lying next to me.

Angels with Clean Faces

(TARA)

I smiled as I slowly opened my eyes and felt Terence's chest against my back and his arm securely draped across my torso. Two years ago, we had one perfect date, but our timing was off. The day after our date, I had left for Australia and when I returned, he had moved to California. Now, here we were halfway around the world, in each other's arms after both of us had fallen asleep still fully clothed.

"Good morning beautiful," Terence said as he leaned over to kiss me softly on my lips. "How are you feeling this morning?"

"Mmmm. Good. I need to get back to my room."

"Do you want me to walk you over there?"

"It's okay. Let me go, get ready, and bring my things over."

After getting up, I quickly went back to my guesthouse and into my room where I took a shower, packed, and checked out. Then, I brought my things over to Terence's room. We went out to grab a bite to eat and headed to a travel agency where we booked a flight to Bangkok that afternoon.

On the flight to Bangkok with Terence, I thought back to the day all of the Nomi Network volunteers had visited the very same shelter where the founders had first met "Nomi." "Nomi" is the pseudonym of one of the young girls who had come to the shelter after having been forced against her will to work in a brothel servicing all the men with sex.

All of the girls at the shelter, like Nomi, had been rescued from similar situations. Nomi's traumatic experiences as a sex slave left her mentally disabled, but coming to the rehabilitation center had given her a chance to rebuild her life. It was this little girl who had inspired Diana, Alissa and Supei to do something to help survivors of sex trafficking. And this is how the Nomi Network was born.

During the visit, several social workers had been on hand to make the girls feel more at ease. They explained to the girls that we were a group of volunteers who had come to spend the day with them, to help them, and to be their friends. For the next few hours, each volunteer spent time with a few of the girls, chatting, reading a book, or playing games with them. At first the girls were reserved and timid, but by lunch, the girls had begun to warm up.

Although these girls had been rescued, we learned that they now faced a number of hurdles. Though they were no longer enslaved, they were now stigmatized and ostracized by their communities. Because of what they had been through, their parents and their community saw them as worthless and disobedient.

Sadly, these girls often felt just as isolated as they had before, when they had been effectively held hostage at a brothel. Many of the girls' families and relatives had turned on them, feeling the shame and judgment of society, but there were a few bright spots. We met a father who stood up for his daughter and spoke on camera saying that she had done nothing wrong, and that what had happened to her was not her fault. A sister of another girl had become a very outspoken advocate, vowing to prevent this from happening to others.

How had these women and girls ended up like this? What were their stories? During the trip, we had also met fifteen survivors who were now young women and with the help of an interpreter, the women shared their stories. A youthful, full-faced woman was the first to share her story. "It was one of our neighbors, an older woman, who asked if I wanted to earn some extra money by working in a restaurant or hotel. Of course I said 'Yes.' It sounded like a good opportunity, better and safer than doing factory work or working in the fields."

In Cambodia, children often have to work to help support their families. The sort of work that Cambodian children did probably violated many child labor safety laws in the United States. We also heard from a young woman with deep set eyes, "One day my mother told me that I was going to go away to work as a maid and that my work would be helping to support the family and to feed my younger brothers and sisters. She told me to be brave and obedient."

Unfortunately their stories were not all that uncommon. Lured into a brothel under false pretenses, and then enslaved, drugged, and beaten into submission, they were unable to escape because they felt trapped and had no idea where they had been taken. Even worse was that in some cases, their parents knew what they were sending their daughters into, but did it for the money. The saddest part was that many of these girls were so young that they hadn't yet reached puberty.

It had been an eventful week of emotional stories. Suddenly, I felt exhausted. I hadn't had a good full night's sleep in the past few days. My eyelids got heavy and I closed my eyes. Before I knew it, the plane had landed in Bangkok.

After clearing customs and immigration, one of Terence's friends, Aran, met us in the baggage claim area and drove us to the inn where Terence often stayed. We checked in, dropped off our bags, and freshened up before we all went out to dinner together. Over dinner, we all got to know each other better. Terence explained to Aran how he and I had initially met.

"We just happened to reconnect in Cambodia, but actually we met two years ago, at a short film festival that I had organized in New York."

"How wonderful that you were reunited by the trip! And what do you have planned for your stay here? What would you like to see? I'd be happy to make any recommendations or to be your tour guide, but I'm sure Terence has that all covered," Aran said looking over at me.

"Actually, I'm mainly planning to volunteer at an orphanage while I'm here," I explained.

"Oh, right, Terence mentioned this to me because he was wondering where exactly it was located. I know the place; it's a few miles outside of Bangkok. It's not easy to get to, so I can take you there," said Aran.

"No, no I was going to take her there," said Terence.

"Come on, you can't take her there on the back of a bike, it's kind of out of the city. Let me give you a lift and drive you over there," Aran said to Terence as he looked over at me.

"Oh, I don't want to trouble either one of you. I can just take a taxi or arrange for some car service to take me there and back," I said.

"Nonsense, let me take care of it. I'll come pick you up tomorrow," Aran said.

Terence looked at me, "Well, you heard the man. Just accept his offer. I know he won't back down."

It was all settled, the next morning Aran was going to pick us up. I was glad that Terence didn't go into all the details or my reasons for wanting to visit the orphanage.

Back at the inn, Terence said, "Let me show you something."

"Okay," I said as he took my hand and we walked past our room, and into the stairwell. We kept walking up to the top floor, and then I realized he was leading me to the roof. There was no one else there, and we had a view of Bangkok at night.

"It's one of Bangkok's best kept secrets," said Terence smiling at me. "I'm so glad that I could share this with you."

I turned to him and smiled as he put his arms around me and we kissed so long that everything seemed like a blur. I had to get up early to be at the orphanage the next morning, so we went back down to our room. As we snuggled in bed together, I felt content and excited, but also strangely relaxed as we explored each other's bodies. Finally, the two of us fell asleep.

Through the Eyes of a Child
(TARA)

The next morning we woke up half-clothed in each other's arms. Terence had offered to go the orphanage with me, but I felt that it was something I needed to do on my own. The orphanage was the one tangible thing I knew about my past. It was the one place that I knew I had lived for a while.

Other than that, there was nothing else I knew for certain about my origins. It was the one knowable piece of the puzzle that I wanted to see for myself. I insisted that he go about his visit to Thailand as he normally would, attending to personal business, and seeing his friends. So he and Aran made plans to go biking together during the day after dropping me off.

As Aran drove us out of Bangkok, the scenery started to change into rural, wide-open land with a smattering of traditional style wood stilted Thai houses. They were immediately recognizable by their steep angled roofs and pointed rooftops.

When I arrived at the orphanage, I walked in and was greeted by a gray-haired man, but I couldn't understand what he said as he spoke to me. I presumed he was speaking Thai.

"Uh, I'm sorry. I don't understand," I said slowly, hoping he'd understand me. "I'm here to volunteer."

"Oh, my mistake, Miss. I thought you were Thai. Are you Thai-American?" he said in perfect English.

"Uh no, not exactly. I don't speak any Thai. I'm looking for Tina," I said.

I had corresponded with Tina a few times over the years. The first was when I was about thirteen years old, and I was curious to know about my biological parents. The second was more recently, after I'd decided to go on the Nomi Network trip. I'd taken a look at the orphanage's website and seen that they had programs for volunteers, so I emailed Tina introducing myself and explaining why I'd like to visit and volunteer. I'd also spoken to her once over the phone.

"Oh, I see. Let me show you to her office," he said motioning for me to follow him.

"Thanks," I said.

He knocked on a door simply labeled *office*, opened the door and said, "Tina, there's a young lady here to see you."

With her hair loosely twisted in a bun, she still looked very much like she did in the photos on the orphanage's website, which were taken fifteen years ago. She was in her sixties now. The only things that betrayed her age were the fine lines around her lips and in the corner of her eyes.

"Hello, you must be Chantara. It's so nice to finally meet you," she said getting up.

"Yes, I'm so glad to finally meet you, too. It's hard to believe that I'm here," I said. Hearing Tina say my full name sounded strange, yet familiar to me. No one had called me by my full name in a while.

I felt like I knew her already. The website told the story of how she been orphaned as a child herself. After she'd gotten married, she wasn't able to bear children. Seeing abandoned children living on the streets, she had started taking them in and eventually opened up her own orphanage.

"Yes, it's so great to have you here. Let me show you around. Who knows, it might even bring back some memories," Tina said with a gentle smile. "Other women, who have come back here as adults, have found that being here brings back memories."

"Oh, I don't know, I was so young when I got adopted, I really have no memory of that time," I replied.

"Well, you just might be surprised," Tina said. "In any case, I hope you find some answers for yourself after this visit."

As we walked around the facility, Tina said, "There are about two hundred babies and children here. We only have a permanent staff of about fifteen people, but we have about sixty regular volunteers who we really count on. This is the nursery."

The room was full of rows and rows of cribs. Some of the babies looked only a few weeks old. A few others stood up, grabbing onto the bars of the crib, looking around, curious about the world around them, beyond the crib.

"Good morning, my dears! How is everyone doing this morning?" Tina said to the women and men tending to the babies. I saw a man was burping a baby over his shoulder, and a woman leaning over one of the cribs was shaking a toy while making cooing sounds. Another woman was straightening things up and cleaning.

"Good morning Miss Tina," they replied.

"I've never seen so many cribs in one room, except maybe in a hospital nursery," I said to Tina.

"Some of these babies' parents simply could not afford to raise them. They came in asking us to look after their children for a few years until they were able to get back on their feet. Sadly, over the years, very few of them have come back to collect their children. I'm not sure if that means that they are still struggling to make ends meet, or if they've passed on, or just moved on with their lives."

One of the babies started crying at the top of her lungs. "Oh my sweet little one, what seems to be the problem?" Tina said as she looked over at the baby. I looked at the tiny baby crying her eyes out. "That's Nisa. She's only a few weeks old, and I think she needs a bit more attention than the others. Do you want to hold her?" Tina reached down into the crib.

"Sure, okay," I said as I wondered if I'd be able to calm her down.

"There's a rocking chair in the corner over there. You can sit with her. Here," Tina said as she handed Nisa over to me. "Don't worry, just relax. She just wants to be held and rocked."

Tina picked up another one of the babies and started singing "Twinkle Twinkle Little Star" very softly as she walked around the room rocking the baby. It worked like a charm. As I rocked back and forth in the rocking chair, I looked down at Nisa who yawned, her eyelids grew heavy and soon she was blissfully asleep. Tina motioned for me to get up. We walked over to the cribs and carefully put the babies back in their respective cribs, and quietly left the room.

"Let's go see what activities the kids are up to today," said Tina as I followed her. "Many of these children were abandoned and so in need of basic human touch and social interaction. When we started out, I worried that we weren't able to give sufficient attention to these children. In the beginning, we had so many friends and neighbors who would stop by to visit, hold, and play with the babies and children. That's when I realized that was the answer, to invite and welcome volunteers to come and spend time with the kids."

As we walked down the corridor, Tina continued, "We also have a number of foreign missionaries who visit the orphanage regularly and perhaps because of this, we get a high number of foreign volunteers—people who happen to be here on an extended vacation or stay. Over time, some of the more regular volunteers have formed bonds and relationships with certain children. And it's worked out. The children have had adult role models growing up and along the way, some of them have gotten adopted. We do also get people who really want to adopt coming here just for that reason."

That's how my parents had adopted me, I thought to myself. I'd been adopted at the age of three.

"Some of the children have been here so long—most of their lives actually and we are the only family who they know. But recently that's changed; the children now stay here until the age of five, then they are sent to a different facility nearby where they can get schooling. We do the best we can to ease the transition." Tina paused, "Okay, so now I'll leave you with Sunny, who is running some activities with the kids here."

"Thanks, it was great finally meeting you and seeing all that you've done for all these kids, and thank you for what you've done for me, too," I said. But somehow the words did not seem sufficient. I felt at a loss for memories that I did not remember.

"Do enjoy your visit and feel free to keep in touch," Tina replied.

The rest of the day was occupied with coloring books, show and tell, and storytelling. I was reminded of how wondrous it is to see the world through the eyes of a child. Some of them had such active imaginations. One little girl in particular, Jaidee, told me all about her little doll Molly. "Her favorite color is yellow. She likes cats but is afraid of dogs."

Another little girl, Rai, mimicked her, "She afraid of dog." Jaidee's English was quite good. Sunny told me that this was because a British couple frequently visited with her, and now they were interested in adopting her. But some of the staff was concerned because Jaidee and Rai were practically inseparable, but since they were not biologically related, the couple was not likely to consider adopting both of them.

The day ended with the children's dinner time at six in the evening. Aran and Terence were already outside waiting for me. Aran had to go back to work at his bike shop, so he dropped us off at the inn. Terence wanted to take a quick shower before grabbing a bite to eat.

Over dinner, Terence and I talked about our days. Terence wanted to know all about how my visit went. After I recounted some of the activities of the day, I said, "I thought that I really didn't have any memories of the orphanage, but being there has unlocked something, I think." I had told him about Jaidee and Rai. "Looking at the friendship between those two little girls, I think that I was like Rai."

"What do you mean?' Terence asked.

"When I was at the orphanage, I remember that I had a best friend, a girl, who was a few years older than me, who I looked up to like a big sister. She really took care of me. We used to play dress up."

"Wow, really? What else do you remember? Do you remember her name?"

"I think her name was... Suki, or maybe it was Sula," I said, pausing, surprised at how much I remembered.

"Tara," Terence said as he reached to touch my hand. "You looked like you were a million miles away for a moment there."

"Oh, sorry. I can't believe all these memories I'm having. When I got adopted and left the orphanage, I remember saying goodbye to her, Sula. She used to say to me, never forget where you came from. Actually, she said it to me in Thai, I think. I wonder if these memories are real and I wonder what became of Sula. She was older than me, I think. Well, old enough to understand a lot more about what was going on at the orphanage. People generally like to adopt babies or younger children, so I wonder if she ever got adopted."

"Did you ask Tina about her?" Terence asked.

"Oh, no, I remembered all this just now, as I was talking to you. I'm not sure where all of these memories are coming from."

"You should reach out to Tina and talk to her about this while you are still here and it's easy to reach her," Terence suggested.

It had been a long day for both of us. Terence told me that he and Aran had spent the day together out in the countryside biking through the back roads in the hot sun.

As we lay in bed together that night, I looked at Terence remembering the first night we met. He was and still is one of the handsomest men I've ever met. He was definitely in really great shape, but he was so much more than just that. Terence caught me looking at him and smiled as he said to me, "Tara, tomorrow is your last day here and the one day for us to spend together in Bangkok. I want to make it special for you."

"Oh, that's so sweet." I leaned over and kissed him. He kissed me back and I felt his hand on the small of my back. He was ready, I was in the mood, and so I said, "I am finding it hard to resist you."

We continued to kiss but then Terence stopped and said, "Tara, I'm not exactly prepared for all this."

"What do you mean?" I asked confused.

"I don't have any condoms. I wasn't exactly prepared or expecting anything like this to happen," explained Terence.

"Oh I see," I said.

Terence had his arms around me, "Tomorrow, just wait until tomorrow. I've planned a wonderful day for us tomorrow. We'll visit some of the temples and sites that I've told you about," he said.

Soon, he dozed off and I lay awake thinking about Tina, the children at the orphanage, and Sula. I hadn't been able to find out anything about my biological parents, but maybe this girl, this Sula, could be the key to understanding some part of my past. Terence was right, I should ask Tina about Sula. I needed to find out if these memories were real at all. That was my last thought as I fell asleep.

Time Stands Still

(TARA)

The next morning I woke up, but Terence was still asleep. I didn't want to wake him, so I went into the bathroom to call Tina. When I emerged from the bathroom after talking to her, I saw that Terence had awakened. "Morning. I didn't want to wake you."

He walked over to kiss me and said, "Thanks babe, I'm going to hop in the shower really quickly."

"Oh, sure, the bathroom is all yours," I said to him.

I started getting dressed and ready for the day ahead. When Terence emerged from the bathroom, I resumed our conversation, "So, before you woke up this morning, I called Tina. She didn't seem surprised at all to hear from me or about the memories I had. It was as if she was expecting my call this morning or something. When I was at the orphanage, she did say something about my visit possibly bringing back memories."

"Oh really?" Terence said as he started looking through his backpack.

I peered into the hotel room safe, making sure that I left behind anything valuable that I wouldn't need today and went through my mental checklist of everything that I'd need for the day.

"I asked her about Sula and she said that the name rang a bell, but she would have to look through all the records that they have there."

"That's great. I'm glad that you talked to her. Instead of just wondering about it," Terence said.

"Yes, now I can relax and really enjoy Bangkok," I said.

"Ready?" Terence asked as he walked toward the door and opened it for me.

"Yes!"

I had read that more than 90 percent of the people in Thailand are Buddhist and that Bangkok had quite a few impressive temples or "wats," as they are called here, so we were going to start off by visiting a few. Aran had lent Terence a motorbike. It seemed like scooters and motorbikes were actually quite common modes of transportation in this part of the world. Terence was quite at home traveling around like this since he had grown up riding around on motorcycles and scooters in Taiwan. He had explained that it would be easier to get around on a motorbike than to drive a car, especially when it came to parking and having to navigate through Bangkok traffic jams.

We started off at the Grand Palace, which was actually a complex of buildings, halls, and pavilions with open lawns, gardens, and courtyards. The first temple we visited was the Temple of the Emerald Buddha. Just as I'd read in guidebooks, there was a sign outside of the temple indicating that shorts or revealing tops were not allowed. I'd brought a shawl to cover up my bare shoulders since I was wearing a tank top. As I fished around for it in my bag, I said, "I bought a shawl, but I can't seem to find it now." I didn't feel it in the bag.

"Oh, wait, are you looking for this?" Terence asked as he pulled out my shawl from his backpack. "I saw it lying on the armchair on the way out this morning and thought you might need it."

"Wow, thanks for noticing! I must have forgotten it in my rush this morning," I said as Terence handed me the shawl and helped me to drape it over my shoulders.

We walked into the Temple of the Emerald Buddha, which was beautifully decorated and I felt a sense of tranquility. It was as if

I were hundreds of miles away from the horrendous traffic that we'd just driven through to get there. The Buddha, which was actually carved from a single block of jade, was displayed high up on platforms. It always feels a bit odd to me, snapping and posing for photos in places of worship, but I snapped a few photos of the Emerald Buddha and the interior of the temple, then Terence and I walked out in silence.

Next was the Wat Pho, also known as the Temple of the Reclining Buddha, which was behind the Temple of the Emerald Buddha. As we walked to Wat Pho, Terence said, "Here's an interesting fact, did you know that it's not uncommon for Thai men to spend some part of their lives as monks?"

"Really? I didn't realize that you could do that—just temporarily be a monk. Don't you have to take some vow of silence or celibacy," I said half-jokingly.

"Oh the vow of silence doesn't apply. But celibacy does apply when men commit to living the life of a monk for a time. Thais see temporary ordination as a rite of passage for men and don't believe that a man is ready for marriage or adult responsibilities until he has spent some time as a monk," Terence explained.

"Interesting. That's some rite of passage especially compared to what we consider rites of passage in America, like prom night, losing one's virginity, being old enough to drink, that sort of thing. How do you know so much about all this anyhow?"

"Actually, I was raised Buddhist and that's why I'm a vegetarian. However, I'm definitely not considering a monastic life. Unlike the Thais, I don't see it as a mandatory rite of passage," Terence said with a smile.

The Temple of the Reclining Buddha is the largest temple in Bangkok. Within it, the Reclining Buddha is more than 150 feet tall and covered in gold leaf. It was gigantic! I stood by the Reclining Buddha and I posed for a few photos.

As we walked out of the temple, Terence said, "They do traditional Thai massages here. Do you want to try one?"

"Sure, that sounds like a good idea."

We decided to do a thirty-minute massage because we wanted to have enough time to stop by the floating markets outside of Bangkok. After putting on a loose-fitting shirt and matching pants, we lay down on mattresses beside each other. I'd never had a Thai massage. I found it to be very gentle and more like a form of stretching. It was as if the masseuse was helping me stretch my legs and arms into some of the yoga positions. After the massage, I felt lighter, like a weight had been lifted from my shoulders.

Next, we headed to the floating markets, about an hour's drive outside of Bangkok. As we sped on the roads outside of Bangkok, the experience was incredible, just the two of us on the bike together, on the open road, with the wind whipping through our hair. The roadside scenery soon changed into the Thai countryside with rice fields, and fruit orchards.

I knew that we had reached the floating markets when I saw a sea of wide, canoe-like boats filled with vibrantly colored, exotic fresh fruits and flowers. There were fuchsia-colored dragon fruit, gorgeous mangoes, wax apples, tropical flowers, and a variety of fresh produce. Terence rented a boat so that we could float alongside the merchants. The floating markets were more than just fruits and vegetables. Each boat was unique. It was more like a floating flea market. Anytime we saw something of interest, we'd drive up to take a closer look. Terence haggled with a merchant about the price of dragon fruit, as I snapped photos.

When we were out of earshot, I said to Terence, "Why did you give that guy such a hard time about the dragon fruit?"

"Oh, that's just a part of the culture. People expect you to haggle. We do that all the time in the night markets in Taiwan," Terence explained.

The smell of fried noodles wafted over, and we remembered that we hadn't eaten lunch yet. A woman in a nearby boat was cooking noodles over a small gas burner, so we flagged her down and ordered vegetable fried noodles. Traffic along the river had picked up with the arrival of tour boats and tourists strolling along the riverbanks.

As we floated by marshes and stilt houses, enjoying all of the frenetic activity around us, Terence noticed a boat with a display of colorful fabrics and silver jewelry.

"See anything you like?" he asked me. "How about a sarong?"

"I usually like to try those sorts of things on, but then I might risk capsizing the boat," I replied.

"Don't worry if that happens, I wouldn't let you drown," Terence said. "Well, they are all one-size fits all and there are many ways to tie it on. I'm sure it will look great on you. How about the one with tropical flowers? Or, maybe, the aqua blue one or the green one?"

I looked over at the sarongs. "Can I see the one with tropical flowers?" The merchant held it up. It was black with several hibiscus flowers printed on it. "How about the aqua blue one?" The merchant held it up and I saw that the fabric was tie dyed shades of aqua blue, royal blue, and green. Oh no, not tie dye, I thought. "I like the vibrant colors of the floral print."

Terence haggled with the merchant once more before handing him some bills in exchange for the sarong.

"Thank you. I love it," I said blithely. "You seem pretty good at haggling. Were you speaking Thai just now?" I asked.

"Yes, but don't be too impressed, I know just enough Thai to be able to haggle," Terence responded.

Soon it was time to return the boat, and head back to the inn since it was already late afternoon and the evening would soon be upon us. Terence had made reservations for dinner and a Thai classical dance show at the Royal T Hotel.

When we got back to the inn, we had just enough time to get showered and dressed. It was nice to be back in our air-conditioned room. Terence handed me the sarong and said, "Do you think you could wear it tonight? Unless, of course, you had something else you wanted to wear. Oh, and you go ahead, take a shower first and start getting ready."

"Thanks, let me see how it looks and if I can figure out how this thing works."

After showering, I fussed with the sarong. I wrapped it around my torso and tied it on the side, then in the front as a strapless number, and then around my neck as a halter. Finally, I settled on the halter-dress style and I emerged from the bathroom with my hair still wet. Terence turned his eyes from the TV and said, "You look gorgeous!" Then he walked over and gave me a quick peck on the cheek as he handed me a red hibiscus flower. "Here's something to put in your hair to complete the look."

While he showered, I blow dried my hair, applied some make up, and put the flower behind my left ear. We took a cab into town and Terence offered me his arm to steady myself as I stepped into a long-tail boat that would take us across the river to the Royal T hotel. By then, it was dusk and the sky was quickly turning into a deep, dark blue.

The hotel was located on the bank of the Chao Phraya River. As we stepped into the restaurant from the riverbank, I admired the touches of traditional Thai décor and the large windows that provided views of the river. Each table featured a vase of orchids. The dishes were as delicious as they looked. They were artfully prepared and a few were even garnished with an orchid or two. Beyond the amazing dining experience, the setting couldn't have been any more romantic.

After dessert, the dance show began. The dancers wore elaborate headdresses and ornate costumes. I marveled at the dancers' grace and their stylized hand gestures. I found myself mesmerized by the curvature of the dancers' hands, which made their fingers seemed elongated.

At the end of the night, we walked out of the hotel to the dock facing the river, which was now quiet and still. Terence held my hand but seemed pensive as we took the long-tail boat across the river, and his quietness continued on the taxi ride home. I wondered what he was thinking. When we arrived at the inn, he opened the door to our room for me. It looked like the room was glowing. Candles had been placed all around the room.

"Oh, Terence, how did you manage to do this?"

"I made arrangements. I wanted this night to be perfect," Terence said as he took me by the hand and led me into the bathroom. Water lilies and floating candles bounced in the large inviting tub. The scent of jasmine filled the air.

"Tara, I can't tell you what it's meant to me to be spending the past few days with you. I'm so glad that we were brought together again. I want you to know that I'm not going to just let you disappear from my life again."

"You'd better not," I said. We kissed. He removed the flower from my hair and gently ran his fingers through my hair. Then, he started kissing my ears and the side of my neck. I closed my eyes as I surrendered to the moment. I could not resist him anymore. We already had three days of foreplay and now I really wanted him.

"Tara, you are so beautiful. I wanted today to be perfect, and this time I'm prepared," Terence whispered in my ear. I slipped off my shoes and he lifted me up into his arms as he said, "Let's go to the bedroom." He carried me into the bedroom and as we stood by the bed, he put his hands around the back of my neck. Then he looked right into my eyes as he asked, "May I?"

I knew exactly what he meant and nodded. He untied the knot behind my neck and slipped off my sarong. I unbuttoned his pants as he removed his T-shirt. Soon, all of our undergarments had been removed and with our bodies now in full contact, I felt his hardness pressing against me. He was definitely as fit as I'd imagined. We began kissing each other with a sudden sense of urgency. But Terence slowed me down and made me wait as he gently ran his hands up and down my body, at first exploring and then touching and kissing me in all the right places until I nearly couldn't bear it.

One moment his touch was so tender and the next it was so firm. I didn't quite know what to expect next. The anticipation was driving me nuts as he kissed and licked my nipples. Then he slowly started kissing my torso and moved down to taste my wetness. I moaned as I felt his tongue and lips on me. When Terence finally entered me, the pressure of him inside of me caused an incredible combination of pleasure, pain, and ecstasy. It excited me even more as he pressed harder against me and I felt his weight on top of me. He reached for my hands, interlaced his fingers with mine and leaned in to kiss me, firmly entering me even more deeply. I closed my eyes savoring the moment as we moved our bodies against each other and continued kissing. Then he released my hands and we started to move into different positions, experimenting with different angles. That's when Terence really pushed me over the edge, to the point that I felt a crashing wave of orgasms like I haven't felt for quite some time.

Afterward, we decided to take a soak in the tub together where we couldn't help but make love again. Then, we moved back to the bed and fell asleep in each other's arms, exhausted by the intensity of our mutual orgasms. That night it seemed like time stood still.

YEAR III

FALL

Not Tempting Karma

(FRANK)

Leah was going to make her annual visit back home to India and she was taking Shanti with her. She would be gone for two weeks and we had never been apart for that long. I kissed her goodbye at the airport, and promised to call her every day. I would miss her but this was going to give me some time to catch up on work. Halloween was coming, and for the first time I wasn't going to pick up a woman at Nine's party.

Wouldn't you know it, the day after Leah left, I received a text message from Speedy. Then a second, then a third. She was in on a layover from London. Her flight crew was stuck in New York due to inclement weather conditions. After the fourth text, I finally responded and asked her to meet me for a drink at the Four Seasons Hotel bar.

She walked in looking as hot as ever, wearing a long trench coat, which made me wonder for a moment, what was underneath. She leaned in to give me a kiss on the mouth and I moved my head to the side so that she kissed my cheek instead of my lips.

"Darling, what's wrong? You have a cold? Is that why you don't want to kiss on the lips?"

"No. It's not that. Have a seat and let's get a drink," I responded.

The waiter came over, and I ordered two glasses of white wine for both of us.

When the waiter left, she leaned in close and said, "You look sexy and virile as always. On the trip here I kept thinking of putting your cock in my mouth and getting you hard, then having you inside me. I don't think I can wait until we get out of here. I think we should just do it in the bathroom of this hotel."

"I wanted to give you this," I said handing her a wrapped box.

"Really? Let me see what is inside." She unwrapped it to find an amethyst pendant. "I like it. Thanks!" She leaned in to kiss me again, and once more I turned my head. She looked confused.

"Speedy, I am breaking up with you. It's crazy to say that since we have never been an actual couple. But I can't have sex with you anymore," I'd said it, plain and simple.

"Why? Why now? Why the gift then?"

"It is a goodbye present. I have a girlfriend now and think I am seriously in love with her. I can't keep screwing you every time you are in New York. I wish you all the best and hope someday when you have a real boyfriend that maybe we can be friends one day."

"Look, I don't care if you have a girlfriend. I won't tell her if you won't tell her," she said suggestively.

"No, baby. You and I have had a lot of good times and you are definitely special to me. But I'm not going to cheat on her."

"Why?"

"Why? I know this may sound strange to you since you have so many guys in so many cities, but not every guy thinks with his dick. Some men don't cheat."

"All men cheat," she said firmly.

"No. A lot of men cheat, but not all men. And, lately, I have been thinking about instant karma a lot. I don't want to stir the pot and mess things up with my girlfriend."

Speedy took the amethyst pendant and threw it in my wine glass, "All men cheat!" she yelled angrily as she got up and left.

I took the amethyst pendant out of the wine glass and cleaned it off.

The waiter came to me and asked, "Is everything okay sir?"

"Everything is fine," I said. "Do you have a wife or girlfriend?"

"Yes, I'm married," the waiter responded.

"Do you think your wife would like this?" I said showing the waiter the pendant.

"Yes, that looks like a nice piece of jewelry," the waiter said.

"Well, then it's yours," I said, "and please bring me another glass of wine."

When the waiter brought me another drink, I sat there for another half hour. Just thinking of all the alleyways and unusual places that Speedy and I had "christened," but I was relieved that Speedy and I had ended. Who would have thought that you actually had to break up with your f-buddy?

It's All About Improvement
(KATIA)

As I walked to Per Se in the Columbus Circle area to meet Addison, I thought back on my life. When I lived in Moscow, in my second year at university, I fell in love with Vladimir. He had just graduated from university and I was very attracted to his looks. He had no money, but he was amazing in bed.

Growing up in Russia, it was all about money. Money means power. There was corruption everywhere and I thought that there must be a better life than this. My life in Russia was like a long, cold winter. Believe me, it is a miserable existence when you don't have money.

Westerners look at me as if I am materialistic. But really, all I have ever wanted is what they have, a chance at a good life. I like nice things and after two years with Vladimir the opportunity for a better life presented itself with Boris. He was twenty-years older than me, and a successful businessman at a natural gas company. We had met through mutual friends and he took an instant liking to me and especially appreciated my face and body. He was going on a month-long business trip to Houston and asked if I would join him.

"Of course, I will pay for the plane fare and you can stay with me in my hotel room," Boris said nonchalantly.

"Do you expect me to share your bed?" I asked.

"Of course, you will share my bed," Boris replied.

"But what about Vladimir?"

"He is a loser. Do you want to be with him for the rest of your life? Think about it. Being my girlfriend means trips overseas, jewelry, furs, fine restaurants. Or, do you want to work like a slave for the rest of your life?" Boris asked in a matter-of-fact manner.

I had just graduated from university and I was at the top of my class, but Boris' offer seemed too good to be true. Even with a good job in Moscow, my life wouldn't be anything like it would be in the West. When I told Vladimir that I was breaking up with him, he reacted with a mixture of anger and sadness.

Boris was used to having his way in life and that also applied to his women. The first time in bed with him, he was much rougher than I thought he would be. He liked to really slap my ass hard and pull my hair when we had sex. He also insisted that I deep throat him and had to swallow. He liked to look at bondage videos on the Internet and kept asking me to wear bondage-type outfits and handcuffs as he barked orders and spanked me during sex.

Finally, after a week of this, I had enough. I packed my suitcase and left him, without even leaving him a note. I was alone, stuck in Houston and I was on a visitor's visa, with no work permit. So, I sublet a very cheap apartment and got a job at a bikini bar where they didn't ask questions about my legal status. Every night men would undress me with their eyes, even though the skimpy bikini I wore didn't really leave much to the imagination. I would smile and chat with them and eventually my tips added up to quite a lot of money.

An older American businessman stopped by the bikini bar and he seemed to stand out in the crowd. His name was Stuart and he looked very tame and the complete opposite of Boris. I also noticed that he wasn't wearing a wedding ring and when I heard that he was from New York, I flirted with him like I have never done before or since, and it worked. He took me back to his hotel room and I gave him the best blow job that he had ever had. He was immediately infatuated with me. He said he would be back in a month. The next time he came back into the bikini bar, we spent the entire week together having lots of sex.

As Stuart and I lay nude in bed, I knew that this was the perfect time to tell him about my situation, "I will have to leave the country very soon. I am in illegal status here. If I go back to Russia, I don't know if we will be able to see each other that much, if at all."

"Back to Russia? That can't be. When will I see you again?" Stuart asked anxiously.

"I know, I want to be with you, but I am afraid immigration will find out about me and deport me."

"Well, if you marry me, then you can stay here legally and come live with me in New York City," Stuart responded.

"Really, you love me that much that you would marry me to keep me with you?"

"Yes, I can't lose you."

He was a nice man and I liked him, but I had no love for him. It was a way to become an American citizen and also to live in New York City. The way I see it, I wasn't using him. I could get any man if I put my mind to it. Stuart had never been married and never had a woman as good in bed as me. He considered himself lucky to have me.

During the time we were married, I worked hard on improving my English. And I took classes to feed my interest in beautiful expensive objects. I studied gemology, antiques, architectural history, interior design, and art history. In the process, I made some high-profile connections in the art world and started to establish my own career as an art dealer.

After a few years of being married to Stuart, I finally got a green card. Not long after that we divorced, but still remain on friendly terms.

I entered Per Se and I spotted Addison immediately. He was just as Luana had described—he looked like he had just walked off of the cover of a *GQ* magazine. I walked over to him; seeing me, he stood up and said, "Luana wasn't kidding. You are a knockout."

I reached out my hand, which he shook. "Thank you. You are quite handsome yourself."

The end of the first date, he escorted me home to the front entrance of my apartment building and I gave him a quick kiss on the lips. Luana was right; he didn't know how to kiss.

"I had a really good time. I hope to see you again," I said.

"Definitely."

Our second date was an evening at Oceana, an elegant seafood restaurant in the Rockefeller Center area. I purposely told Addison that I always wanted to visit the U.S. Virgin Islands. And he got the hint. The next weekend, we both checked into a room at one of the most expensive hotels in St. Thomas.

The first night in bed, I was very happy with his muscular body. As he started pecking me like a bird, I slowed him down and put my index finger on his lips.

"Addison, I like the way you kiss, but can I teach you how I like to kiss?"

"Of course, that would be great," he responded.

We spent an hour kissing slowly. Each time he tried to peck my lips, I showed him how to move his lips and how to kiss slowly and sensually. He had been hard all this time, and so I decided to whisper in his ear.

"Please lay back and let me do all the work. I want to show you how I like it," I said in a lusty voice.

Addison laid back and I put a condom on him. I removed my panties, got on top of him and slowly started rocking back and forth. When he started to do some jerky movements with his hips, I stopped him.

"No honey. Follow my lead," I instructed.

I thrust my pelvis back and forth slowly at first and told him to match my movements. I could see that he was having an aha moment as he saw how much I was enjoying myself. A huge grin came across his face, and I could tell that he now understood how to move his body with mine. After five minutes, I came. Not a fake orgasm like I used to have with Boris or Stuart, but an intense one like I used to have with Vladimir. I was really turned on by Addison. He already had the looks and a great body, but now he knew how to kiss and make love.

We would go shopping on our dates. We went to all of the upscale stores on Fifth Avenue, Madison Avenue, SoHo, the Meatpacking District, and others. Anytime I found something I liked in an expensive store window, Addison would buy it for me. It didn't matter how much it cost. Whenever he had a weekend off from work, we went on a trip to some expensive resort.

I met with Luana over brunch and I told her all this. She was happy to hear how successful I had been with molding Addison into the man I wanted him to be.

"I haven't seen him since that one night we had together. It's amazing how you've been able to come up with a new and improved version of Addison," Luana remarked. "I never would have been able to have the patience to do what you did."

"I need to keep a good eye on him now. He is a real catch now."

"Are you starting to have feelings for him?"

"Yes, I am. He is everything I ever wanted in a man," I said surprising myself at what I just said.

Alternate Reality

(NINE and Montoya)

Montoya, Joy, Kristof and I were seated at a corner table in Fiorella's, an upscale Italian restaurant, thanks to Kristof who had made a reservation for us. Located directly across from Lincoln Center, it was packed since a new opera was premiering that night.

"Now, this is a miracle. I had never been on a double date but lately it seems to be becoming the norm," Montoya remarked.

"Hey, with God all things are possible," Kristof said.

"So, where were you two earlier today?" Joy asked Kristof and me.

"We were at the Museum of Natural History and saw the sky show at the Hayden Planetarium," I responded. "I could spend hours at the Hayden Planetarium. When they turn off all the lights and when the stars fill that auditorium, I feel like I'm being taken away to outer space. When I was a teenager, I wanted to be an astronomer and I read every book there was on astronomy. But when I got to college and struggled with my first calculus class, I realized my dream wouldn't happen."

"Well, it did lead to your love of sci-fi," Kristof said.

"Yes I love sci-fi novels which are usually something reserved for nerds, but to me, they open up a whole world of possibilities. One of the things that intrigued me was the idea of parallel universes. What if, in another universe, I was already married and had children? What if at every fork in the road I had taken, the road led to a different path than what I actually have here. How would my life look different?"

"I for one am glad that you are with me in this dimension and reality," Kristof said as he kissed me on the cheek.

"So am I," I replied smiling back at Kristof. "He is like my rock of Gibraltar. I have never dated a Christian guy who had more integrity than he has," I explained.

Joy gave Montoya a sideways glance with a smile on her face.

"Hey, I resent that," Montoya quipped.

"I didn't say anything," Joy said looking tickled.

"Mr. Perfect over here makes all the rest of us guys look bad," Montoya said nodding at Kristof. "Joining the engaged couples' class after only a few months of dating is a very strong statement."

"As my mother always told me, when you find the right person, you will just know it. Both Kristof and I know we are right for each other and we both want the same thing. Being in the engaged couples' group is the right thing for us to do. We wanted to start things off right. As we grow into our relationship together, we want to learn how to navigate life together. We know that this isn't going to just be some fly-by-night romance," I said confidently.

"Other people in the engaged couples' group couldn't believe we were in the class and not engaged yet. Actually, it's The Journey Church's 'pre-marriage' counseling group and it makes you discuss many topics most people don't normally talk about," Kristof said as he grinned.

"Why that big smile?" I asked Kristof.

"Montoya and I got together for a man-to-man talk and he gave me some very good advice," Kristof said.

"What advice did Montoya give you?"

"I told Kristof that he was going to have to work on his tele-pathic skills if he wanted to be serious with a woman—especially with someone like you, Nine. So, I helped him out a little bit," Montoya said.

"I think it is better that I show you," Kristof said as he got up from the table and got down on one knee in front of me. I gasped and my mouth dropped open.

"Nine, even though it hasn't been long since I have known you, when you know, you know. I know that in this reality or any other reality that we are meant to be with each other. I don't want to wait another moment to let the world know that you are the only woman in the world for me." Kristof pulled an engagement ring out from his jacket pocket and held it out for me. "I love you with all my heart. Will you do me the honor of marrying me?"

Tears immediately streamed down my face. I leaned over and put my hands on his face and gave him a huge kiss.

As our lips parted Kristof asked, "So, is that a yes?"

"Yes! Yes! It is a Yes!" I said laughing and crying at the same time.

As Kristof slipped the ring on my finger, several of the patrons at Fiorella's clapped and cheered. Joy hugged me and Kristof. Montoya congratulated both of us, shook Kristof's hand while he patted him on the back, and then gave me a kiss on the cheek and a big hug.

Just then, a thought crossed my mind so I turned to Kristof and asked, "Did you talk to my parents about this, specifically my Dad?"

"Yes, I did. I spoke to them on the phone and arranged to meet with them in D.C. one Saturday afternoon. I took the Amtrak there and we all had lunch together. They appreciated that I was asking for their permission and approval. Your Mom said that she thought that I had demonstrated good old-fashioned manners. Your father also seemed pleased, although he did mention something about a firing squad if I ever cheated on you."

Hearing this, Montoya commented, "A firing squad? Knowing General Anderson's Air Force combat background, I would've thought a high altitude drop without a parachute would be the preferred method of dealing with a cheating son-in-law."

I laughed at Montoya's comment and said, "No one is killing anyone. By the way, Montoya, was it your advice for Kristof to propose?"

"I told him to make a grand gesture. My suggestion was to not be the only couple in the engaged couples' group who wasn't engaged," Montoya said.

"And I told him your ring size and helped him to pick out the ring," Joy added.

"You and Joy are the best!" I almost screamed as I hugged Montoya and then Joy.

I admired the ring I now had on my finger. "This ring is exquisite."

"It is a two-carat diamond surrounded by four emeralds," Kristof said proudly.

"I love emeralds!" I responded.

"I know," Joy added with a knowing smile.

"I'm not sure what life I'm living in some parallel dimension, but this one just got dramatically better," I said beaming.

One Scoop or Two?

(TARA and Roxanne)

Anita was a friend from work and she had told me all about Barry; how sweet, thoughtful and caring he was. Surprisingly, he wasn't the artistic type that she usually goes for. Barry was an actuary and Anita said that there was just something about him. She was already thinking that he could be the one. Anita had a Friday night ritual of going out dancing with her friends. That's how she had met Barry.

"You should join us, and you can also finally meet Barry," Anita had said inviting me to join them. "Besides, we haven't gone out at all since you got back from your trip to Cambodia."

"That does sound like a lot of fun. I haven't been dancing in a while," I said thinking that I could use a fun night out of dancing. I was also a little curious about Barry.

We were to meet at the club Kiss and Fly. On the way there Anita texted me that she and her friends were at the bar in the main room. I didn't know any of Anita's friends. When I arrived and found Anita, she hugged me and she whispered in my ear, "You have to tell me what you think of him."

Barry was not at all what I had expected. He definitely was not the type of guy that Anita usually went for. The first thing I noticed was that he was not tall. Anita is already quite petite, and Barry was not much taller than her. I shook Barry's hand and said, "It's so nice to finally meet you. I've heard so much about you."

"And I feel like I know all about you too," Barry replied. Something about the way he had looked at me as he said this made me feel odd but I couldn't put my finger on it.

Soon I was on the dance floor with Anita and her friends who were getting their groove on. We were a sizable group of fifteen. It was the first time I'd been out dancing since returning from Cambodia and Thailand. And it felt great as I surrendered to the music. Throughout the night the cast of characters on the dance floor changed as people rotated on and off the dance floor. But about half of the group always seemed to remain on the dance floor. I remained on the dance floor the entire night without taking a break. I felt unstoppable as I closed my eyes and moved to the beat of the music. At some point I looked around and realized that none of Anita's friends or Anita was in sight. I was left alone on the dance floor with Barry and a bunch of strangers.

Barry moved toward me to dance with me. Then, he extended his hand offering to take my hand in some sort of a partner dance. Barry held my hand in his and put his other hand around my waist. He held his hand up to indicate that he was going to twirl me around. I twirled under his hand and he did this a couple more times, back and forth, back and forth. I felt a bit light-headed afterward, as if I had just been spun around like a top.

Then, he let go of my hand and started dancing behind me and that's when he lifted his right hand and brushed it across my right boob. It startled me but I thought to myself, maybe it was an accident, but then he did it again with his right hand. As I smacked his hand away he reached over with his left hand and cupped my left breast. I smacked Barry's left hand away, turned to him and said, "Excuse me? What are you doing?" And, then, I just walked off the dance floor because I didn't want to make a scene. I didn't know what to do. I just felt like I wanted to go, get out of there and just disappear and leave. I didn't want to have to face Anita or her friends. As I left, I texted Anita saying that I was leaving because I had a bit too much to drink and was going to call it a night. I wasn't sure what to do about the whole thing.

When I got home I couldn't stop thinking about it. Should I try to tell Anita about Barry? If Anita really thought that Barry could be "the one," didn't I have a responsibility to tell her what had happened? If the roles were reversed wouldn't I want to know?

The next day Anita called me and asked, "I was wondering why you left so suddenly last night. Were you trying to avoid some confrontation?"

I was a bit taken aback and thought, how did Anita know? Had someone else from the group seen what happened? "What do you mean?" I asked her.

"Barry told me what happened on the dance floor."

"He did?" I said wondering what would make Barry confess.

"Yes and I am glad he did. I never expected this of you, of all people!" Anita said raising her voice and sounding upset. "How could you do this to me?"

"What are you talking about Anita? Barry made a pass at me."

"I can't believe that you are trying to blame him. Maybe in your twisted mind you thought he made a pass at you, which would make it okay for you to grab his ass and hump him on the dance floor. From what I understand, there was some stroking going on too."

"That is ridiculous, Anita! I would never do that. I know you are not going to believe me but you have it all wrong. It was the other way around. He made a pass at me. He grabbed my boob. That's why I left so suddenly," I said trying to explain but feeling as if it my words were falling on deaf ears.

"Barry told me the exact opposite—that you grabbed his ass and stroked his dick, but then when he told you to stop, you stormed off.

How am I supposed to believe you? I don't know what to believe. I just wanted you to know that I know about this. I wanted to put it out there before I see you at the office on Monday. Let's not make any scenes at work." And then Anita hung up the phone abruptly on me.

I was pretty distressed by the conversation with Anita, so I called up Roxanne to talk about it. First, I explained to Roxanne what had happened. "We were just dancing and it seemed harmless enough. When you're in a loud dance club it's usually just easier to keep dancing than to talk. It's so loud in clubs."

"Sounds innocent enough so far," Roxanne said.

"Well at some point we were dancing and Barry brushed his hand across my boob! He was standing behind me and he raised his hand and clearly brushed it across my boob."

"Are you sure that it wasn't just an accident? Maybe he was doing some dance move and your boob got in the way? Or his arms just got out of control," Roxanne said trying to make light of the situation.

"Very funny. Right, it was my boob that crashed into his hand. The first time I was just a little startled and yes, I thought maybe it was an accident. But then he did it again and I tried to slap his hand away. He didn't take the hint and tried a third time—it was very deliberate. He cupped his hand underneath my breast. It was clearly a scoop. So, that was it, I just walked right off the dance floor."

"That does sound quite deliberate," Roxanne said.

"Right. I'm not just a piece of meat to be manhandled. I guess I could've slapped him, but that's not my style and he was a friend's boyfriend, not just some random lecherous guy. I wanted to slip out without having to say goodbye to Anita, so I just texted her that I was leaving. I just couldn't face Anita. I mean even though we are just co-workers, she has become a friend. We've talked about girl stuff, hung out outside of the office and I like her very much. And I see her practically every day at work."

"That does sound like an awkward situation," Roxanne said pausing. "So are you going to tell Anita about what happened with Barry?"

"Well, actually, she called me first," I responded.

"Oh really? Was she suspicious of something?" Roxanne asked.

"Yeah, but it's not what you think. Get this, her boyfriend claimed that I grabbed his junk!"

"What? No way!" Roxanne exclaimed.

"Yes, he claimed I was stroking his dick on the dance floor! Can you believe it?! He got to her first and turned the tables on me. I tried to defend myself but she wouldn't believe me. I mean really? Did she really think that I would or could really do that? I wanted to tell her that it was really the other way around—that it was her boyfriend who made a pass at me. But there was no reasoning with her. She'd never believe me."

"That is a bad situation since you need to see her every day at work. If Barry is the type of guy who likes to make passes at women, your friend Anita will find it out soon enough without you debating about who did what," Roxanne said reassuringly. "His true colors will come out soon when he makes passes at other women. Until that time just be polite and professional with her at work."

The following week I decided to try to get through to Anita and to tell her the truth again. My opportunity came that week when everyone in the office decided to go out for farewell drinks. It was our colleague Ron's last day. Ron was well liked and the whole department was planning to go to a nearby bar for drinks. I knew that Anita would be there. It had been awkward between the two of us all week, but at the bar Anita seemed different. Ron was talking about his wife's second pregnancy and their plans to move into a big house in New Jersey. Toward the end of the night, Anita and I found ourselves sitting at the bar, just the two of us. Ron and most of their colleagues had already left. It was like old times. That's how we had actually first bonded—over drinks one day after work.

Anita broke the ice first, "I'm really happy for Ron. He's such an upstanding guy. It really makes you think that there are still some decent men left out there."

"Yeah, they're still out there. Anita, I really hope you believe that I would never do anything to get in between you and Barry. I would never make a pass at him. I really want to straighten things out with you about that," I responded.

"Well I didn't really know what to think. I didn't think that Barry would lie to me about something like that and make up such a story," Anita said with a tone of resignation.

"I know this might be hard for you to believe, but I really didn't make a pass at him. He's the one who actually made a pass at me," I asserted.

I told Anita about "the scoop" and Anita's demeanor changed immediately. "Well, actually we've broken up," Anita said with tears in her eyes.

"Oh Anita I'm so sorry to hear this. I wanted to tell you what happened because I thought you should know, especially since you said that maybe he was 'the one.' I know if I were in your shoes, I'd want to know. So what happened between you two?"

"I was such a fool. I was blinded by love. I was so crazy about Barry. I thought that he was a catch and that, of course, other women would see that. That's probably why I thought you might have made a pass at him," Anita lamented.

"Seriously Anita, I really wouldn't do that, I mean he was your boyfriend," I said.

"It turns out that what Barry did to you, he also did to my friend Sue. We were at some crowded dive bar when Sue screamed at him so loudly that everyone in the bar including me heard her. I was so mortified that I broke up with him on the spot. I'm so sorry about Barry's behavior. I couldn't imagine that he could do something like that, but now I know what he's capable of."

I was relieved that I had told Anita about what had happened and glad that Anita had found out on her own about Barry. However, I was not entirely sure that Anita would have believed me otherwise, but at least we had finally cleared the air. Now, Anita knew the truth. The conversation could have just as easily gone the other way, I thought. It's not always easy to tell someone the truth since you never know how they are going to take it.

The Toy Chest

(LUANA)

I ducked under the awning of some café in the West Village and waited for the rain to pass. That's what I get for not checking the weather in the morning. It was autumn already and I had dashed out the door without an umbrella. As I watched people rushing about in the rain, I thought about Taylor, who used to live in this neighborhood. A few years ago we had gotten caught in the rain together on this very same street.

Taylor had said, "I only live two blocks away. Come over to my place and we can change out of our wet clothes. I will lend you some of my clothes so you have something dry to wear."

"That sounds like a great idea. I am drenched," I replied.

We ran the two blocks in the pouring rain to her apartment building. Comfortable and unpretentious, her place was filled with throw pillows and scented candles. As both of us started removing our wet clothes, I noticed Taylor checking me out. I realized that I had never been naked in front of her.

"Luana, you look great, but now that I can see what's been underneath your clothing, I have to say you have an amazing body. I think I have a good body, but I just can't compare to your definition and tone. You must work out like a mad woman," Taylor said admiringly.

"Yes, I've always been fit. It makes me feel good and I love it when guys admire my body. As they say, 'vanity is sanity.' "

Taylor handed me a towel and said, "If you want to take a shower, the guest bathroom is over there. And if you're not in a hurry, let's relax, have a glass of wine, and watch a movie until it stops raining."

"Sure."

"There's a robe in there—if you want to put something on when you're done. I'm going to shower in my bathroom," Taylor said as she walked into her room.

I emerged from the bathroom wearing the little satin robe that I'd found in there. Taylor was wearing an oversized T-shirt and not much else.

"Take a look through my DVDs and see what you like," Taylor said.

As I looked through her DVD collection, I saw one that got my attention. "*Basic Instinct*. I haven't seen this one in about ten years. I love the scene where Sharon Stone crosses and uncrosses her legs. Talk about a woman taking control of a situation using her femininity."

"That's a good one," replied Taylor as she got us both glasses of red wine and some cheese and crackers.

As she bent over to put the DVD in, I could see that she was not wearing any panties. Was she flashing me? I must admit that she was a very sexy woman with curves in all the right places. She sat next to me on the sofa and as she leaned in and slowly poured me a glass of wine, I could see right down her T-shirt. I knew what she was doing since I had used the same moves myself to seduce men. Her loose fitting white T-shirt didn't leave much to the imagination. In fact, that was all she was wearing. When it came time for the famous Sharon Stone scene, Taylor put her hand on my bare leg. All I had on was the little silky robe. When I looked at her, she gave me a lascivious smile.

"This is a good scene," Taylor said. "Can you do what she did?"

"Of course."

"Show me," Taylor challenged.

I got up and sat in an armchair across from her, and then I crossed and uncrossed my legs seductively, knowing that she could see up my robe.

"I like what I see," Taylor said, her eyes lingering over me a bit too long.

She walked over to me and slowly untied my robe, looking at me to see my reaction. Without even thinking about it I smiled back. "Mmmmm," the sound escaped from my lips as she began licking my nipples and simultaneously stroking my inner thighs with her hand. She kissed my shoulder and then kissed my neck and earlobe. I played along to see how far things would go and to see what would happen. She knew what she was doing.

As she kissed me on the mouth, her kisses became more and more passionate and intense until she had one hand caressing my boob and another hand in between my legs. She knew right where my G-spot was and how to pace everything. The way she was touching me, few men have been able to do. I found myself giving in to her. Soon, she was going down on me. It was one of the most powerful orgasms that I've ever gotten orally. I could definitely see the appeal of women for men. Their bodies are so soft, and skin so touchable.

It turned out that Taylor was bi, but I had no idea because I had only seen her with guys. I tried it with her for about a month, and it was different, especially when we dug into her "toy chest." She had everything. The first time, she used a strap-on with me, it was as intense as any orgasm I'd had with a guy. I got into using all different types of "apparatus," but I just couldn't seem to get into giving oral sex to her. I really didn't enjoy it. I'd always make sure that I satisfy the men I'm with, but in bed with women, I am selfish. I would rather they go down on me.

The other thing was that although Taylor was a "free agent" if you get my drift, she was very possessive of me. I realized that I could not deal with that. How could she expect me to be exclusive with her, if she was not going to be exclusive with me? We remained friends after we broke up but I made sure we never crossed that line again.

Recently we saw each other at a mutual friend's party. There was some underlying sexual tension and flirtation between us, but it was our own little secret. Being with women is different and fun, but ultimately, I just like men's equipment better.

Men, You Can't Live With Them or Without Them

(LUANA)

Finding a really good lover is one thing but finding a good lover who also can be and wants to be a good father is like trying to win the lottery. Any man can *father* a child, but being a *dad* is an entirely different story. Would the father of my child be a *dad*, in other words, would he be there for the diaper changing, midnight feedings, school plays, dance recitals, or PTA meetings?

What makes a good father for your child? I think that most women want these basic qualities in a would-be father—someone kind, caring, and responsible. We ladies really want someone who looks like a male model and who has the qualities of a good father.

I'm not so sure that I want a husband though, since I have already done the marriage thing. After Miguel and I got divorced, he decided to go back to Brazil and I moved to New York City to make a fresh start and it has been quite a ride! I've never had any trouble meeting men and have never been alone for very long.

For some time, I have been thinking about trying to have a child again. I've been out with some men who I thought had the maturity necessary to be a good father, but they seemed so old that I was afraid that they might die of a heart attack while we were in bed together. I work out seven days a week, so to have sex with me; the man really has to be able to keep up with me.

Then, I thought about just having a man around for sex and asking him if he'd like to father a child. That would be fine. I would handle the rest of the responsibility. I started dating very young men in their early twenties, well at least twenty-five, that seemed like a good age, and not too young.

I met Gabriel, a very charismatic, blonde graduate student studying for his Ph.D. in economics at New York University. He was very fit and I found out why; he enjoyed swimming and playing squash and tennis. Soon, we became lovers, but we were really more like friends with benefits. He told me that he had been married once. He had married his high school sweetheart before he even finished college. Now, he wanted to be free to experiment and experience other women. I had been thinking about asking him to father a child with me, but with no strings attached.

Gabriel was working on a big research paper, so knowing that I wouldn't be seeing him, I went off to a wine tasting. There I met a good-looking, blonde man, Michael, who was from Iceland, but trust me, there was nothing icy about him. He was quite a hunk and very young. He told me he was twenty-four and had recently graduated from law school. I liked him immediately. In the middle of our conversation, he got a call from his office about some legal case he was working on and had to excuse himself. It happened so fast that I forgot to ask him for his business card or to offer him mine. And, then, I didn't see him again that night.

So, I decided to try my luck with the "missed connections" on *Craigslist*. I sent the following message:

> We didn't get a chance to exchange business cards or phone numbers tonight, so I am trying to find you here. I am the hot brunette in her 30's and you are the hot blonde man in his early 20's. If you see this, please respond back. Would be good to get together for a coffee.

I got back this response:

> I think I am the one you are looking for. I definitely think you are who I am looking for. We met briefly tonight at David's bachelor party. We had talked about going to a swinger's party sometime soon and I called you a dirty, dirty girl. How about proving that to me now and giving me a call :)

At the end of the message was a phone number to call. *Ai, me deus do ceu!* I can't believe this crap! I immediately recognized that the cell phone number belonged to Gabriel. So, instead of working on his research paper, he went to a bachelor party and met a brunette in her thirties at the same time that I met Michael, the hot blonde man in his twenties. He must have thought that my *Craigslist* ad was from this woman.

I know that Gabriel and I were not exactly exclusive, but seriously, what are the odds of this mix-up? I took it as a sign that this relationship was not meant to be. So I forwarded him the email message in response to my *Craigslist* ad, which I knew was actually from him. Then, I texted him telling him to check his email. He called me immediately, but I let his call go to voicemail.

"Luana, someone must have hacked into my computer! Not sure how that happened! Trust me, I would never do that to you!" he said in his message.

I didn't respond. He emailed me and texted me multiple times over the next two hours. I still didn't respond.

The next day, he sent a dozen roses to my office, but I didn't respond. Did he really think that I'd be dumb enough to believe him or to forgive him? Besides, whomever was going to be father to my child had to be smart enough to realize that I had written that ad myself, which meant that I was trying to reach out to another hot blonde. Eventually, the emails from Gabriel stopped.

Michael never did respond to the "missed connections" ad I posted. Right now, I'm thinking, I will be better off with a sperm bank donor to father my child. Who needs a real father for my child? I make enough money. I just need a hot man for sex. He can keep his sperm.

Doing It Without Doing It

(LUANA)

I've done a lot of things by myself—moved to New York, bought my own place, and made a new life for myself here. I have a good job, great friends, and I have no want or need of anything. But I do realize that what I really want is to have a baby. I'd love to have a little girl. I am ready to take another chance at becoming a mother.

But up until now, I haven't found the right man. Life is too short to go through a life sentence of misery with someone. Having been through one divorce is enough. It's definitely not something I want to repeat. I have been with guys and wondered, what if I "accidentally" got pregnant? I'd want to keep the baby but not necessarily the guy, but I knew I wouldn't feel right knowingly keeping this information from a man.

If I was going to keep this information from the father of my child and raise the child myself, well, that wouldn't be much different than just getting pregnant by a sperm donor. So lately I've been thinking, why wait? I can afford it... So, why not just buy myself the one thing I want, but can't do all by myself?

These days, it's as easy as 1—2—3. You can shop for anything on the Internet, including a sperm donor. Believe it or not, it's all out there and the list of sperm donors is available for free. It's even easier than online dating. You don't need to sign up, fill out any lengthy questionnaires, or pay any membership fees. You can look up donors online for free in the privacy of your own home and search based on any criteria at all—ethnicity, educational background, age, height, or blood type. Some donors want to remain anonymous. Others are open to having communication with the children they've fathered. You can see what his hobbies and occupation are, and even if he has fathered any other children.

The donor I picked was Puerto Rican, a graduate student of French literature, who did rock climbing as a hobby. He seemed like someone sensitive, intellectual, and adventurous. He had also indicated that he was open to being contacted by his donor children in the future. I just hope he doesn't end up unknowingly fathering a hundred different children. There have been cases of sperm banks doing this and men later discovering that their sperm had been used to father anywhere from seventy to one hundred children.

I decided to literally "do it myself." It could have been done in the doctor's office, with a speculum, and a syringe, which sounds kind of like a visit to the gynecologist, doesn't it? Seems like a very impersonal way to make a baby. Yes, getting pregnant from a sperm donor seems impersonal. That's why I thought at least I'd try to do it in the privacy of my own bedroom. I wanted it to be as pleasurable an experience as possible. I'd read somewhere that having an orgasm during intercourse, and also presumably when getting inseminated, could improve the odds of getting pregnant.

Certainly there are many good reasons for having a doctor do it. The doctor can test your hormone levels, do an ultrasound to monitor your egg production, and give you an injection or a pill to increase your egg production. All of that will up your odds of getting pregnant. I was prepared to go that route if doing it myself didn't work.

So, I arranged to have a frozen vial of sperm delivered overnight by courier right on time, at the height of my ovulation. I let it thaw at room temperature for a bit as I slipped into a silky satin robe with nothing else on underneath it. Then, I turned on some soulful

Latin music and once the contents of the vial had thawed, I filled the syringe and warmed it to body temperature with my hands.

I went into my bedroom and placed the syringe on my bedside table. I lay down and got comfortable as I let my robe slip open. The fragrance of the candles in my room enveloped me. Lying on the bed, I slipped a pillow under my hips to elevate them and began touching myself, letting my hands wander and slide up and down the sides of my torso, I closed my eyes and imagined some of the most extraordinary lovers that I've had, the modern dancer with the perfectly sculpted body, young lovers with marathon stamina, older men on Viagra who were so eager to please... I've been with them all... stereotypes are just that, stereotypes.

What they say about Asian men is not true—what you see is different from what you actually get—when he's ready that is—catch my drift? As a matter of fact, I have been with Asian men who were huge and black men who were small. I prefer girth to length, but both are necessary. Whether a man is circumcised or not, or pierced down there, doesn't affect how good he is in bed. Carnivores don't always have the strongest libidos and vegetarians don't necessarily taste the best. I have really seen it all. I was going through a parade of sex partners in my mind and just as I was getting turned on, I reached for the syringe and injected its contents deep into my vagina. I continued to stroke myself until I came. Feeling relaxed, elated and exhausted from the release of tension, I fell asleep.

I dreamt that I was walking through a forest. Somewhere in the distance I heard a baby crying. I tried to follow the cries. As I got closer, the cries got louder and then they stopped. I didn't know where the sounds were coming from—in the dream I wondered if I was imagining it or actually hearing it. And then I woke up.

In the following weeks, I swear that I had all the signs. I felt bloated, my breasts felt tender, and I was a bit more tired than usual. I couldn't wait, so I went to the drug store to purchase a home pregnancy test. I rushed to get home to use it, but when it came out negative, I was crushed.

After my period came, I made an appointment with my ob-gyn to discuss having the artificial insemination procedure done in a doctor's office. The fertility specialist suggested that I take a fertility drug at the beginning of my menstrual cycle before undergoing the procedure. That was to be followed by an ultrasound to determine when I'd be ovulating so that we could time the procedure.

Postscript: When I finally got the good news that I was pregnant, I was so overjoyed, but decided not to share that information with anyone. I was going to wait until after the first trimester. After all I've been through, I just want to keep this as private as I can and not make any public announcements until I'm absolutely sure.

YEAR III

WINTER

Gentlemen Prefer (   )?

(TARA)

Minh and I were at Maru in Koreatown. It was a futuristic, modern space with white walls and purple lighting, which made the place look like the oversized interior of a Virgin Airlines plane. The entire time, Minh had been observing a guy dressed in a brown sports coat at the other end of the bar. All night he had been trying to chat up several women without much success. He was now trying to strike up a conversation with a petite Asian woman who was standing by him. It seemed like the woman was more interested in getting the bartender's attention than in talking to the man.

Always sharp and direct in her opinions, Minh turned and said to me, "See that guy in the dark jacket across from us? He has 'yellow fever.' All of the women he's been trying to approach tonight have been Asian."

The man in question was white and looked like he was in his mid-thirties.

I looked over and said, "Oh really? What's the big deal? Everyone has his or her preferences. Some men like blonde hair and blue eyes, some like big girls and big booties, others like petite women or dark skin and dark hair."

"But you have to admit, there is such a thing as an Asian fetish. There are some men out there who think that Asian women are exotic; yet, they don't really know anything about Asian culture. To me, that's just kind of creepy and disturbing." Minh paused and then continued, "When I went to Beijing University for a semester on an exchange program, there were a number of American male exchange students also in the program and I saw how they went after the Chinese female students."

"Yeah, but I'll bet that your Chinese classmates were not exactly fighting these guys off," I pointed out.

"I'll have to admit that a lot of Chinese girls, well actually, I think that a lot of women in Asia have 'white fever' and practically fall all over Caucasian guys."

"So, I guess stereotypes can work both ways with Asian women, especially the ones living in Asia thinking that Caucasian men are somehow exotic and different," I added.

"It just doesn't sit well with me when people seem to have a specific preference for a particular ethnic group," Minh said as she looked across the bar. It looked like the petite Asian woman had finally gotten her drink. She took her drink and tried to slip away unnoticed from the guy who'd been trying to chat with her. As she started walking away, he turned to say something to her, but she kept walking and disappeared into the crowd. Obviously, he had struck out with her.

"Yeah well, you never know where people are coming from, what motivates them, or why they are interested," I replied.

"Well, I want to know that someone is genuinely interested in me," Minh responded. "What I also find annoying is when guys say things like 'konichiwa' or 'ni hao' to me. Especially, when they say it like 'kooonichiwaaaah!'"

"Ni howdy ladies!"

Minh and I turned to see the man in the brown sports jacket standing right before us. I giggled and Minh looked annoyed, so the man said to me, "Oh, you get the joke, I really meant 'ni hao.'"

Here we go, I thought, as I saw Minh roll her eyes. Seeing Minh's reaction he said, "Oh, maybe I should be saying 'koooni-chiiiiwaaah…' "

Minh turned to him and said something in Vietnamese and then in Mandarin to him as she batted her eyelashes at him.

"Uhmmm. Translation please," the man responded.

"Ni hao, konichiwa? Why even use those words if you don't speak Mandarin or Japanese?" Minh responded.

"I was just trying to start a conversation with you two ladies."

"I understand. But what makes you think that those pickup lines, which by the way are not exactly all that original, would work on us?" Minh asked. "Do you think using those lines to pick up Asian women is really respectful?"

Listening to Minh, I had to admit that it was so typical. She and most Asian women in New York have probably heard these phrases from some random man in a bar or as they walked down the street.

"Don't look at me. I can't speak a word of either language," I said.

"You know what you're doing is actually kind of offensive," Minh continued.

"Wow, you ladies are a tough crowd!" the man responded some-what defensively.

"Look, this is my public service announcement for the night. Do yourself a favor and try to approach Asian women with something more original. Just be yourself," Minh offered.

"Okay, I think you made your point," the man said and then walked away.

"Okay, that guy was a bit odd," I said. "But, still, I don't think all non-Asian guys who end up going out with Asian women have 'yellow fever' or an Asian fetish. You've dated non-Asian men, who aren't like that, haven't you?" I asked.

Minh reflected a moment, "Yes, I guess I just don't like men who are so obviously going after Asian women with such flimsy tactics. I don't want a man who is interested in me just because I am some kind of novelty. I definitely prefer Asian guys over non-Asian. Sometimes, it's more about what you feel comfortable with. I'm more comfortable with Asian or Asian-American guys. I think that we are just more culturally similar," Minh said.

"Well, I didn't grow up around many Asians at all. I'm pretty open about dating either Asian or non-Asian men," I said and then added, "Somehow, I haven't really dated all that many Asian men, not because they haven't approached me. And it's not that I'm against dating them."

"Well, at least you're not one of those girls who says she's not attracted to Asian guys," Minh said.

"It's never worked out with any Asian guys, well, until sort of recently," I replied.

"Oh, right, this new guy, Terence, is Asian."

"Yeah, he's Taiwanese. We've been keeping in touch, but I'm not sure what to expect or where this is headed since it's long distance," I said.

"Long distance relationships are so hard, but in the meantime, you've got to still get out there and have a life, like you are right now."

I knew that Minh was right. I knew better than to get too single mindedly focused on a man at the expense of my friendships.

"I guess what happened with that guy earlier just bugged me because I don't want someone to like me just because I'm Asian. I don't want to be objectified. That's the problem. I mean it would make me wonder if I'm just one of the many, indistinct Asian women that a guy could be dating. If so, I don't think I'd feel that special," Minh said.

I could see where Minh was coming from, "Yeah, you definitely wouldn't want to be dating a guy who was so superficial that he didn't look beyond the surface. But maybe you'll never really know if that's the reason why a guy went after you in the first place. And so what if that's what attracted him to you initially? Just as long as that is not the only thing. You should also be able to trust your instincts to help you evaluate why a guy is interested in you and if he really respects you."

"I still prefer Asian guys," Minh said.

"Yellow fever, white fever, call it what you will. Deciphering whether someone is into you just because of your skin color, hair color, or measurements is not always easy, though that may be what attracted someone to you initially. Let's hope that it's about something deeper since looks will fade and hairs will go gray," I concluded.

Grow Up Already

(ROXANNE)

I was in a rush. I had taken a little too long to get ready and was now running late. It's funny how a dress that's made you look and feel completely fabulous in the past could, on some other day, just seem not quite right. I was having one of those days. A closet full of clothes but nothing seemed to work. After trying on a few things, I decided to go for the tried and true, a little black dress. However, when I put it on, it just seemed to lack some oomph. After scouring my closet, I discovered my royal blue dress. It had been one of my favorites but I'd forgotten all about it. This dress was a classic and always made me feel good. It showed off my curves without being too revealing and brought out the blue in my eyes.

The air was chilly as I stood on the corner of Central Park West and 59th Street. It was much colder than I'd expected. I stuffed my hands into my coat pockets and hunched over bearing the cold, waiting for the light to turn. A white kid dressed in a jean jacket carrying a backpack stood beside me, with his hands in his pockets hunched over mimicking my mannerisms. Noticing him out of the corner of my eye, I turned to look over at him as he said:

"It sure is cold tonight. So where are you going? Can I come along?"

The light turned green.

"You're funny kid," I said as I stepped into the crosswalk. He was just a baby-faced kid. I looked over at him wondering how old he was.

"You're not going to tell me? Maybe I'll just follow you then," the boy said as he walked alongside me.

"Oh, be my guest," I said while laughing inside. What would the kid do once we arrived at a bar where he'd be carded and not allowed to enter?

"So, I guess I'll just follow you home and then we can get in bed together and cuddle?"

"In your dreams kid. Don't you have somewhere you should be going?" I said, feeling a bit uneasy.

"Oh, there's the subway station. I'm going to take it home," the boy said walking off in the distance.

What was that all about? How random, I thought. I was not sure how to feel about the whole thing. It was seriously odd. I did attract younger men sometimes, but this was ridiculous.

My thoughts turned to Oliver who I'd met a few weeks ago at a speed dating event at the Penn Club in midtown. Now, he was a man with a capital "M." Mmmmm, mmmm, mmm.

The flirtation between us had started that day immediately when Oliver had said to me, "I find people fascinating. You think you know someone but then you realize that you really don't."

"What do you mean?"

"Well, I only recently discovered that one of my friends, who I've known for years doesn't like chocolate."

"Who doesn't like chocolate?" I had said suggestively in response to Oliver. He had laughed, getting the subtext of my comment.

He was gorgeous, and from the limited time I had spoken with him, it was obvious that he was very well read and full of all sorts of trivia. Oliver's complexion and facial features reminded me of one of my friends, Vince, who was part African-American and part Native American. But Oliver was definitely cuter. He also had this delightful little dimple, which appeared on the left side of his face each time he smiled or laughed. I love men with dimples. I've always had a weakness for them.

At the end of the speed dating event, we ended up being a mutual match, and were given each other's contact information. So, we continued to correspond via IM and email. Oliver had teased me about what my favorite type of chocolate was. Soon, we were discussing everything from reality TV to art history. He seemed like the type who could talk with practically anyone about practically any subject. Maybe I had met my match.

As I arrived at the bar, my thoughts turned to seeing Oliver again. I stood there scanning the room looking for him, but he was nowhere to be found. Suddenly, I heard a man's voice calling, "Roxanne."

I turned around to see a wiry young man with freckled skin, red hair, and horn-rimmed glasses. At first I was confused, then I realized where we had met. "Oh hi. Were you at the singles speed dating event two weeks ago?" I said slowly, trying to conceal my disappointment that he wasn't Oliver.

"Oh, don't pretend that you don't recognize me. I love your sense of humor. I'm Oliver. We met there and have been exchanging emails ever since. I was so glad that you agreed to meet again," he said, his voice cracking. "Come join me. What would you like to drink?" Oliver motioned to a seat at the bar where there was a glass of beer.

"I'll have a glass of your house red, thanks," I said now remembering that there had been two Olivers at the end of the speed dating event. Obviously, there had probably been some sort of mix up with the contact information that I had been given. Realizing that I had actually been emailing and IMing this other Oliver, I decided to stay just to see where things would go. He was not at all who I was expecting to see. But we had some meaningful discussions over the past few weeks. Fishing for clues to jog my memory about our conversation at the speed dating event, I asked him, "So, I was wondering, what was it about what I said or what we talked about at the speed dating event that made you want to see me again."

"You said that you were lonely and desperate, and I decided to take pity on you," Oliver said, his voice rising and falling like an adolescent boy's.

"Excuse me?!" I said wondering if this was his lame attempt at humor. I was not amused.

"But seriously, you remind me of my ex-wife," Oliver said as the pitch of his voice rose and fell. "And I have a weakness for blondes."

I felt as if I was dealing with a prepubescent boy. I raised my glass and took a big sip, "Now, that doesn't quite sound like a compliment."

"Oh, come on. Don't be like that. I brought something for you," Oliver said, his voice cracking.

Oliver took something out of his jacket pocket and handed it to me. It looked like a chocolate bar except that the outer wrapper, which would have had the brand name on it, had been removed.

A Ghirardelli bar would have been nice. I wasn't even expecting a Lindt bar. But this chocolate bar, I didn't know where it had come from. Just when I had thought, this date could not possibly get any worse, it did. Who gives someone a chocolate bar that looks like it's been already partially opened without an outer wrapper? I handed the chocolate bar back to Oliver. I was not impressed.

"What? You don't like it?" Oliver said, his voice squeaking. I thought you really liked chocolate. You said a few times in your emails how much you like chocolate. You said you didn't necessarily have a preference for dark chocolate."

"Listen, Oliver. I don't think this is going to work out. I thought you were someone else."

"I don't get it. I'm the same guy you met at the speed dating event and that you've been emailing these past two weeks."

"No, I mean I thought you were someone else completely different, even while we were emailing each other these past few weeks. There's been a mistake. I was expecting to see someone else entirely today," I said feeling annoyed. "I'm sorry, but I have to leave now."

I slapped a 20-dollar bill on the bar as I got up to leave. I couldn't sit through any more of this, listen to Oliver's voice, or wait for it to change. As I walked toward the subway, I thought, what was up with all the prepubescent boys today? One had literally tried to pick me up and then I had found myself on a date with a man who sounded and acted like a prepubescent boy.

Two Condoms are Better than One
(FRANK and Montoya)

Montoya and I were having beers at Hooters in midtown. A football game was playing on several of the flat screen TVs around the bar, which was packed with several groups of men, and a few couples. Some seemed to be on a date and others appeared to be married. Several waitresses dressed in little orange shorts and tight Hooters T-shirts were dashing about the restaurant taking orders and bringing customers their food and drinks. A buxom brunette brought us a large order of chicken wings.

"Seriously, I can't believe how hard it is these days to find some free time that doesn't involve spending time with Leah or Shanti," I said while reaching for a chicken wing. "It is amazing how we had the time to go to all those parties and mixers."

"Indeed. Now I have to do really good time management to be able to work on my screenplay. Lately, I've been thinking about quitting my job and devoting all my time to making it in show business as a screenwriter and movie producer. Remember how I told you about Vonnie, the former centerfold? I'm thinking of working on something with her, but then I would have to explain my history with her to Joy," said Montoya.

"Speaking of women who require some explaining… I recently got a call from Speedy."

"Oh your shag buddy?"

"Yeah. I decided to end it once and for all, so I actually broke it off with her."

"Good for you mate," Montoya said.

"What about your Greek goddess?" I asked and then added, "That's the person that I think you should be more worried about than Vonnie."

"I wouldn't risk what I have with Joy. So, when Melina is in New York next year, I just will have to tell her that I have a serious girlfriend and can't be her shag buddy anymore," Montoya responded. "Did you tell Leah about Speedy?"

"Hell no! That's in the past," I said taking a swig of beer. "Also, I wouldn't recommend meeting with Melina in person unless you really have to."

"For a long time, you and I both went around having sex like it was a sport," Montoya said.

I smiled at the thought and added, "And man, did we have fun doing it."

"It seems like wherever I go, I run into women I know and somehow this always happens when I'm with Joy. Once I was on the subway with Joy when I saw my friend Dina and as soon as she saw me, she came over to give me a warm hug and kiss. She's eight-months pregnant. Joy gave me this curious look as Dina was kissing me. So, I said jokingly, for Joy's benefit and right in front of Dina, 'It's not mine! I know her husband and I went to their wedding,' " Montoya shared.

"When you really think about it, it is amazing how many women we have dated in Manhattan," I responded.

"Only Manhattan? I think I'd include all five boroughs, and the bridge and tunnel crowd," Montoya joked as he grabbed a handful of French fries. "It's a wonder we can still stand."

"Speak for yourself. Remember, I was out of commission for three months while doing physical therapy. And having to walk around with a cane didn't exactly help me with picking up chicks. So, I guess you picked up my slack," I kidded.

"It's a tough job but someone had to do it," Montoya wise-cracked. "But now I'm definitely retired."

"Thank God, Leah isn't the jealous type."

"You are a lucky man! But really, I couldn't blame a woman for being a bit jealous knowing about my past exploits. So, the idea of working closely on a movie with an ex, who also happens to be a former centerfold, may not be the brightest idea I've ever had—especially now that I have a girlfriend."

"Funny. Speaking of not so bright ideas, remember my two-condom trick? I always try to wear two condoms whenever I have sex with a woman because condoms are not reliable. And having an extra condom on is like having a spare parachute when you go skydiving. Lately I actually have been thinking about something that was unthinkable only a year ago. I was thinking of ditching the condom with Leah."

"No! I don't believe it! You want to have a rugrat with Leah? And, I thought my religious experience in Jerusalem was a miracle," Montoya said stunned.

"Yeah, being a Christian now, you should be the one being 'fruitful and multiplying,' " I said laughing.

"What about marriage?" Montoya asked.

"Now, that is scary! Much scarier than having a kid."

"I am the exact opposite. I can see myself marrying Joy sometimes. However, having a baby and being responsible for changing diapers is not something that I look forward to. Besides, I don't want to be one of those dunces who walks super fast on the sidewalk pushing along a baby carriage and is ready to run over whoever is in his way.

I don't get that. You see these people zooming through the streets with a baby carriage like they are driving a Mack truck. What is the hurry? If you don't jump out of the way, it's as if they will slam the baby carriage into you. It's plain reckless."

"Hey, I might become one of those baby carriage speedsters. So, don't knock it 'til you've tried it," I said with a laugh.

"So, no condom at all?"

"Well, I am down to just one condom these days. The thought has occurred to ask her if she wants me to not wear one."

"Well, I have heard everything now. It is scary what some women will do to have a baby. I've heard stories of slipping the condom off when they are having sex or giving the guy a condom that they stuck a needle in. But a man who wants to slip off the condom, not the woman... that's a first, especially coming from you, of all people."

"The idea of having a kid appeals to me a lot. It's like a part of you that lives on after you are dead and buried," I said.

"Books or children? That was the ancient maxim about people wanting to leave something of themselves as a lasting legacy. For me, I would like it to be the movies I write or produce. However, if Joy and I do get married and she wants to have a kid, I would do it for her. I won't be selfish about that."

I raised my beer mug in the air. Montoya also did. "To movies or children, whichever comes first," I toasted as Montoya and I clinked our beer mugs.

Who Needs a Storybook Wedding?

(Nine, Montoya, Tara, Luana, Frank, Katia and Roxanne)

Nine and Kristof decided to get married on Valentine's Day. Nine thought that it would be the perfect day to celebrate their love. She had many relatives coming in from Germany and various parts of the United States. Many of her relatives had never been to New York City before, so she made arrangements for them to go on special tours of the city. Highlights would include visiting Central Park and several major museums, going shopping on Fifth Avenue, and at several major department stores, as well as taking in some Broadway shows. That was the plan. However, you might say that planning a wedding is kind of like planning a war. Nothing ever goes totally according to plan.

The soon-to-be newlyweds had picked a very large Presbyterian church on the Upper East Side for their wedding. Nine's parents flew in from D.C. a week before to help with all of the preparations. Her father, General James Anderson, looked especially commanding, dressed in his military uniform. Now in his early sixties, he had maintained a muscular physique from his early days of military training. Only his salt and pepper hair betrayed his true age. Nine's mother, Astrid, had light brown hair and green eyes. She had maintained the same slender figure that had attracted then Leiutenant Colonel James Anderson. One could see how much General Anderson still adored his wife from the endearing way he looked at her.

A few days before the wedding, it began snowing so heavily that some of the guests couldn't fly into JFK, LaGuardia, or Newark in time for the wedding. On the day of the wedding, it also snowed heavily, and some of the guests had difficulties driving into Manhattan.

Nine had asked Montoya to be the best man and Kristof, in turn, had asked his older sister Ann to be the matron of honor. Nine also invited Joy to be one of her bridesmaids. As Joy and Montoya waited for the ceremony to begin they chatted.

Montoya was sharing his thoughts on weddings and marriage. "I have a theory. I believe that perfect, storybook weddings, are just too good to be true. Having a storybook wedding doesn't guarantee that there will be a 'happily ever after.' My thought is that it's not perfection that people should be striving for on their wedding day. Maybe, it's only natural that something goes wrong at your wedding."

"Are you kidding? Are you just waiting for something to go wrong with Nine's wedding?"

"Well, yes, actually. It is similar to how actors say 'break a leg' on opening night. It would be incredibly bad luck to wish an actor 'good luck' before his or her performance. So, if you dream of a storybook wedding, you are just setting yourself up for disappointment, if not outright failure. Case in point, my friend Brooke had a wedding where the wedding photographer accidentally left the lens cap on his camera during the entire filming of the wedding. They thought they were getting a bargain for the price he charged. They got incompetence instead of a bargain and had no wedding photos, at least not official ones. But they have been married for twenty-five years."

"That is really warped thinking!" Joy responded.

"Well, my dear, it's a metaphor for marriage and life, which is not always picture perfect. If you can weather the stormy conditions, then it's smooth sailing ahead. I am just sharing my thoughts. Hey, let's go check on the bride." Montoya and Joy went to the prep room in the back where they knew they'd find Nine.

They knocked on the door and Nine's mother opened the door for them. Nine was on the phone.

"Oh, my God! Are you okay? Your right arm is broken? My God. No, don't worry about me. Take care of yourself," Nine said almost yelling.

"What happened?" Montoya asked after she got off the phone.

"You're not going to believe this, but the wedding photographer was taking a cab to get here and the cab skidded in the snow and got into a horrible accident. He was calling from the hospital emergency room."

"I heard. A broken arm," said Montoya.

"What am I supposed to do?"

"Look, I know several heads of networking organizations who routinely have photographers at their events. Let me make some calls. I am positive someone is available," Montoya reassured her.

But it was Tara's friend, Joanne Louie, who found a photographer who was available. She found Charlie who usually photographed her networking events. So, problem solved. As wedding problems go, this was a very minor problem. Then, Nine got a text message. The wedding singer had laryngitis and couldn't sing. She could barely talk and had to send a text message to Nine. So, Luana enlisted Sophia, who was among the wedding guests, to ad lib something. Still, no biggie.

The rest of the wedding went well without any hiccups. Kerrick, the minister at The Journey, officiated and when he said, "I now pronounce you man and wife" the audience went into thunderous applause.

At the reception, it seemed like Nine had invited half of The Journey Church to her wedding. The rest of her guests were from all the mixers and parties she had frequented in Manhattan. In attendance were Roxanne and Katia with her new boyfriend Addison. Frank brought Leah, and Tara showed up alone. Luana, now three-months pregnant, was still flirting with every good-looking man in sight.

Tara spotted Luana and walked over to her saying, "Congratulations, beautiful Mama!"

"Thanks! I am really hoping for a girl, but I will be happy just for the baby to be healthy," Luana said as she gently caressed her tummy.

"I saw you talking to some of the gorgeous men here. I guess you're not going to let pregnancy cramp your style," Tara said amused.

"Yeah, I was talking to that hunk over there," she said as she pointed across the room. "I told him I liked motorcycles and horseback riding... hint, hint."

"I take it he didn't get the hint," Tara said.

"No. Not at all. He's some serious eye candy, but unfortunately dumb as a doorknob. I told him about how I liked baseball, football, basketball, and he says, 'Oh I guess you like sports.' I said, 'No Mr. Genius. I like balls. Get it? Balls,' " Luana said laughing.

Frank and Leah joined them, as did Katia and Roxanne.

"So, Luana, I guess getting you drunk now is out of the question?" Frank said smiling.

"Frank, you do realize that she can't drink alcohol," Leah interjected.

"Let me tell you guys, lately it seems like I've been meeting real duds, so I'm glad I haven't waited around to find a daddy for my baby," Luana said. "I was on a date with this guy named Murray about a month ago. I still wasn't showing at all at two months. Well, this man was about the most obnoxious man I've been on a date with. He brought me to an expensive restaurant but as I was I ordering my food, he started peppering me with questions about Brazil. He kept asking me about past leaders and facts about Brazilian history, and for every answer I got wrong he would go 'Ehhhhhhhhh' like the sound of the buzzer on *Family Feud* or *The Price is Right*. It was so ridiculous, that I got up and just left."

"You mean after you had eaten your food?" Roxanne asked.

"No, I had ordered my food, but I just got up and left before it even arrived. No goodbye. He was a jerk."

"You should have at least gotten an enjoyable a meal out of it," Katia added.

"No. His cross-examination was unbearable. I am so glad I decided to have a baby on my own," Luana asserted.

Roxanne started to also share a story of one of her recent dates. "I was riding on the monorail between terminals at JFK airport when this man asked me out. He was cute, so I told him I would think about it. When we did meet for dinner, I have to say that he was boring as all hell, but at least the meal was really good. So, I agree with Katia, you should have at least stayed for the meal."

Montoya came over and said, "Nine and Kristof are about to make their big entrance."

The newly married couple (Mr. and Mrs. Eklund) walked into the reception hall to roaring cheers and applause. They sat at a long table that had been prepared for them and the rest of the wedding party. After the emcee introduced the wedding party and everyone was seated, it was now time for Montoya to make a toast and to give the best man speech. He stood up and raised his glass.

"Hello everyone. Half of you are already pissed drunk, while the other half of you may have to wake up early for church tomorrow, so I will keep this very brief. I started out as Nine's mentor at work and then we developed a truly wonderful friendship. Now, she has become my mentor when it comes to relationships. Nine and Kristof, I wish you all the happiness in the world and I know that you two will be a very happy couple!" All of the guests raised their glass and toasted the happy couple.

A few toasts later, toward the end of the meal, Frank walked over to talk to Montoya. "Good job with the speech."

"Maybe you are next?" Montoya said directing the all-important question to Frank.

"Listen, you crazy Brit. Those are fighting words," Frank said chuckling and clenching his hand in a fist, mocking that he was going to hit Montoya. Instead, the two gave each other a hug and a pat on the back.

"I do have some big news for you though. I talked to the Managing Partner for New York at my law firm and starting Monday I am going to start working reduced hours as a Counsel at my firm. This will give me more free time to work on writing the screenplay that I keep talking about."

Frank was surprised, "I'm happy for you! But what does Joy think about this?"

"I have to do it now, before I get married and maybe have kids to worry about supporting financially. Joy supports my decision."

"Thanks man, for letting me know. Looks like you are starting off on a new life as well," Frank noted.

"It's time to cut the cake!" the emcee announced. Nine and Kristof got up and walked over to the cake table and posed for the flashing cameras as they cut into the cake and fed each other a piece of it. Then, they walked onto the dance floor and danced their first dance.

As their song ended, the DJ called on other couples to join them. Then, Montoya and Joy got up and made their way to the dance floor, followed by the other groomsmen and bridesmaids.

Tara smiled as she saw Montoya and Joy on the dance floor and then Frank and Leah. As she took a sip of her champagne, she heard a familiar voice say "May I have this dance?" She turned to see Terence standing behind her holding a red hibiscus flower.

"Terence! I thought you weren't able to make it!" Tara said as she put down her glass of champagne.

Terence handed her the hibiscus and said, "For you, my dear." Tara put it behind her ear as Terence continued speaking. "I had a change in plans, but by then I figured it was too late for you to RSVP for me. So, I thought I'd surprise you instead." He reached out his hand to Tara. She took it and stood up to put her arms around him. They kissed and embraced, and then he led her to the dance floor.

Nine was bursting with happiness. She had forgotten about the problems with the photographer and the singer. She and Kristof were smiling and greeting all the guests who soon filled the dance floor.

"So, this is the lucky guy," Frank said to Tara as he and Leah danced nearby.

"Yes, Frank, this is Terence," Tara said. "Terence, this is Frank and Leah."

Montoya and Joy had also noticed Tara on the dance floor, as did Nine and Kristof. Roxanne was dancing nearby with a black guy dressed in a military uniform. "Terence, this is Montoya and Joy, Nine and Kristof, Roxanne and…" said Tara.

"Leo," said Roxanne's dance partner.

Nine looked over at Roxanne and smiled as she said, "Roxanne, I see you've met my cousin, Leo."

"Hi guys, it's nice to finally meet you all," Terence said. "Congratulations to you," he said as he looked at Nine and Kristof. "I'm glad to meet all of you—at last!"

When they were finally "alone" and out of other's earshot, Terence leaned into Tara's ear and said, "I have another surprise for you. I'm moving back to New York!"

Tara couldn't believe her ears. At first things had fizzled out between Terence and her when he moved to California; then, they were reunited in Cambodia. But she wasn't sure how she felt about being in a long distance relationship, given what had happened with Sebastian. "How did this happen? When?" she asked.

"Well, I knew that I didn't want to be in a long distance relationship with you and I couldn't bear being apart from you, especially after how close we became in Cambodia and Thailand. So, I was looking for opportunities to return to New York. And, it just so happens that one of my friends is going to be starting his own documentary film production company in New York and he's invited me to be a part of it."

"That's so exciting! It's your dream job," Tara said as she hugged him, and then they kissed.

Suddenly, they realized that the music had stopped and the emcee was asking people to clear the dance floor for the bouquet toss, "Could everyone clear the dance floor except for the single ladies?"

When the bouquet was thrown to the crowd of women, Nine threw it a bit too far and it landed right at the feet of Luana who wasn't even standing with the group of women who were trying to catch it.

Seeing this, Katia said to Luana, "Maybe the universe wants a real father for that kid?"

The Burning Bush

(NINE)

We left for the start of our honeymoon immediately after the wedding—giving me just enough time to do a quick change of clothes out of my bridal gown.

I don't like long flights, so we decided to do an overnight layover in London. Then, the next day we would fly to our honeymoon destination of Israel and Egypt. After the trip with Montoya, I knew that I had to go back there one day, and I wanted to share the experience with Kristof.

The flight from JFK airport to London seemed like the longest flight of my life. This was it! I was finally going to be with Kristof. As we watched a movie on the flight over, I couldn't stop thinking that I had just gotten married to this man. Married!

A few years ago I wouldn't have been able to imagine that everything would turn out as it has. Montoya, the ladies' man, was now a Christian in a serious relationship with Joy. Frank had also found love with Leah, Tara too with Terence, and Luana was now pregnant. It seemed like the wild ride of New York City's dating scene was coming to a close for all of us. Going back to my alternate reality theory, I wonder if it could actually be any better than this in some other dimension.

Kristof and I checked into a big suite at our hotel in London. He carried me through the doorway of the hotel room—like they do in old-fashioned black and white movies. As soon as Kristof tipped the bellboy for helping us with the luggage, and we were finally left alone, I was all over him. I started kissing him up and down his body with his clothes still on. He started unbuttoning my blouse revealing my sexy black lacey bra. As I started unbuttoning Kristof's shirt, he had started removing my bra and soon he was gently kissing my boobies. Then, he picked me up again and carried me to the bed. Laying me on the bed, he spread my legs and started kissing me between my legs while I still had my skirt on.

"Undress me," I demanded feeling giddy.

Kristof complied and removed my skirt revealing a skimpy thong that matched my lacey black bra. "Wow, this was definitely worth the wait," he said as he continued kissing me in between my legs and peeled off the thong. I was nude on the bed but he was still wearing his pants, which I saw now had a bulge.

"Take off your clothes," I ordered him with a smile.

Kristof took off his clothes and lay on the bed next to me. He started French kissing me and then kissing my neck and earlobes. He turned me around on my stomach and started kissing me all over my shoulders and back and then kissed both of my butt cheeks. I had heard about and read all about making love, but actually feeling and experiencing Kristof's touch and bare body against mine for the first time was beyond words.

Now, it was his turn to give an order. "Lie on your back."

I lay back as he got a towel from the bathroom and put it underneath me. Then, he put a condom on. I was ready for him, but still it took a little effort for him to ease himself inside of me.

"Wow. That is tight," he said.

We started French kissing passionately as we had many times before, but this time, for the first time, he was actually inside me. I felt my body moistening and receiving him as he gently and slowly moved deeper and deeper inside of me, gradually filling me up. As I moved with Kristof as he started to slide himself in and out of me. I had gotten orgasms before from men using their tongues or their fingers, but this orgasm was different. It made me light headed, but in a good way. He continued to press his hardness deep against me until he was finished. We were both finished. "I'm dead. You killed me," I said to him.

There was some blood on the towel from Kristof breaking my hymen. But that was to be expected. Kristof removed the towel and got some tissues to clean both of us. Then, we lay in each other's arms and fell asleep. When we woke up, we had worked up quite an appetite so we showered together and went out to dinner. During dinner, I looked at Kristof and thought, we are now husband and wife in every sense of the word. Neither of us could wait to get back to our room and go at it again. We did make love again. Immediately after, we fell asleep and soon we were jolted awake by our alarm.

In the morning we hurriedly got dressed, checked out, and rushed off to the airport, just making it in time for our flight to Israel. As we touched down in Tel Aviv, I felt a wave of happiness.

On the first day, we spent hours on the beaches of Herzliya and Tel Aviv. The next day we went to a Dead Sea resort. The water in the Dead Sea isn't like any other water on planet earth. You have to climb over rocks to a point where you can go deep in the water and then you float... yes float. It is impossible to drown in this water, since it really isn't water per se. It is oily water mixed with a large amount of minerals.

There's such a high concentration of oil in the Dead Sea that if you don't put Dead Sea mud on yourself, you will literally fry and get sunburned. It is an odd sight, seeing people walking around covered in mud from head to toe. Kristof and I slathered sea mud on each other and it was actually kind of erotic. We spent the next few days at a resort in Eilat where there were great beaches and snorkeling. The underwater sea life was so vibrantly colorful and beautiful.

Despite danger in the region from recent events, the next part of the honeymoon was in the place I've always wanted to visit, the Pyramids of Egypt. I felt okay because I knew that we had many people from The Journey praying for us to have a safe honeymoon. The flight to Cairo from Tel Aviv was short. From what I've seen on television, you'd think that there are only three Pyramids, but actually there are several smaller ones surrounding the three big ones in Giza, which is very close to Cairo.

We paid an Egyptologist to give us a private tour of the Pyramids. With all these Pyramids, there's actually only one that allows the general public to enter. As you walk in you must bend over at the waist just to get in through the doorway. Another pyramid had a big hole in it, from when a British general tried to blow it up in search of treasure. What an idiot! The Sphinx was amazing and less weathered by the centuries than I thought it would be. We rode around on camels in the Pyramid area and I discovered that they really stink.

In Cairo, so many people were praying in the streets, and prostrating on little mats. It made me realize that everywhere you go, there are people who are devout in their religion. Next, we took a brief cruise down the Nile River. What I didn't expect was to see some dead animals floating in the river. Needless to say, after that, I only drank bottled water for the rest of the trip. Our final destination was Sharm El-Sheikh. We spent the day snorkeling in the beautiful water. The underwater scenes were as stunning as those at Eilat.

Close to our hotel was St. Catherine's Monastery in the Sinai desert. The monastery was built on the spot where the Roman Catholic Church believes that Moses spoke one-on-one with God. There is actually a bush that is supposed to be "The Burning Bush."

It was bigger than I thought it would be and amazingly, the rocks surrounding it have the image of the burning bush fossilized on them. It was surreal.

As I stood at the burning bush for a while, I thought about my life. I gave thanks silently to God for all he had done for me. I felt very close to God and had tears in my eyes, but they were tears of happiness. I am glad I waited to give up my virginity to Kristof. Only now, in hindsight, I realized it was worth it.

On the flight back to New York, I thought, I am Kristof's wife now. I know that marriage takes a lot of work, but I'm ready.

End of Year III

EPILOGUE

As William Shakespeare once wrote, "The course of true love never did run smooth." So what makes for a good romantic relationship anyway? For Nine it was finding a Christian with integrity. For Montoya, it was finding someone who inspired him to be a better person. For Tara it was finding someone who shared a humanitarian cause she believed in, for Frank it was someone who could be elegant to the public but wild in private, and for Katia, it was someone who has deep pockets of cash. But not everyone needs a romantic relationship. For Luana, it was finally deciding she didn't need a relationship to have a child. Each of us is different and there is no one-size-fits-all model.

Nine and Montoya met Kristof and Joy through church. Tara was reunited with Terence on a humanitarian trip. Frank got to know Leah gradually over the course of several months, as he was going through physical therapy. And Katia met Addison through the introduction of a friend. There are plenty of people who will sleep with you in Manhattan, no matter how attractive or unattractive you are. To paraphrase a line from the classic movie *Casablanca*, "We're shocked, shocked to find that sleeping around is going on in here!" But to make a real connection, it really takes time and the right circumstances to get to know someone.

We wish all of you, our noble ladies and esteemed gentlemen, the best of luck in your relationships. As the Bard would say, "Now our revels are ended."

But are they?

ABOUT THE AUTHORS

Felicia Lin is a Taiwanese American writer who was born in Fairbanks, Alaska and raised in Ottawa, Ontario, Canada. She has a bachelor of science degree in Accounting from the University of Illinois at Champaign-Urbana and a master of arts degree in Applied Psychology from New York University. Currently, she resides in New York City. To learn more about her visit: www.felicialin.com.

Victor Scott Rodriguez is a native New Yorker, born in Brooklyn, and raised in Brooklyn, Queens and Manhattan. He has a bachelor's degree in Communications from Hunter College, a bachelor's degree in Religion from Rutgers University and a master of arts degree in Divinity from the University of Chicago Divinity School. Currently, he resides in New York City. To learn more about him visit: www.victorscottrodriguez.com.

Find Out What's Next for Metropolicks

VISIT www.Metropolicks.com

JOIN our mailing list to learn about events, news, and special offers.

WATCH us on  YouTube.com/user/Metropolicks

LIKE us on ❢ Facebook.com/Metropolicks

FOLLOW us on  @Metropolicks

CONNECT with us on in Linkedin.com/company/ Metropolicks

PIN us on ⑫ Pinterest.com/Metropolicks

FOLLOW us on  @Metropolicks

DISCLAIMER OF ENDORSEMENT

Reference contained in this novel to any specific commercial products(s), service(s) by trade name, trademark(s), manufacturer(s), organization(s), institutions(s), corporation(s), the appearance of external hyperlink(s), church(es), place(s) of worship or otherwise, does not necessarily constitute or imply its endorsement, recommendation, or favoring by any of the heretofore referenced or any governmental agencies. The views and opinions of the authors expressed herein do not necessarily state or reflect those of those commercial product(s), services(s) by trade name, trademark(s), manufacturer(s), organization(s), institution(s), corporation(s), the appearance of external hyperlink(s), church(es), place(s) of worship, governmental agencies or otherwise, and shall not be used for advertising or product endorsement purposes.

Neither of the authors has financial interest by the reference to any specific commercial product(s), services(s) by trade name, trademark(s), manufacturer(s), organization(s), institution(s), corporation(s), the appearance of external hyperlink(s), church(es), place(s) of workshop or otherwise nor has any specific commercial product(s), service(s) by trade name, trademark(s), manufacturer(s), organization(s), institution(s), corporation(s), the appearance of external hyperlinks(s), church(es), place(s) of worship or otherwise, paid any monies to the authors to be referred in the novel.

www.ingramcontent.com/pod-product-compliance
Lightning Source LLC
Chambersburg PA
CBHW050947120626
46552CB00001B/430